Fiction International 45
"About Seeing"

Fiction International is a journal of letters and arts published at San Diego State University. *Fiction International* was founded, published, and edited by Joe David Bellamy at St. Lawrence University from 1973 to 1983.

Business correspondence, including that related to subscriptions and advertising, should be directed to:

Harold Jaffe
Editor, *Fiction International*
Department of English
San Diego State University
5500 Campanile Drive
San Diego, CA 92182–6020

E-mail: hjaffe@mail.sdsu.edu

The views expressed herein are those of the authors, not the editors or sponsors.

Printed in Canada

Microfilm and xerographic copies of out-of-print volumes are available from:

University Microfilms International
300 North Zeeb Road
Ann Arbor, MI 48106, or
3032 Mortimer Street
London W1N 7RA, England

Fiction International is abstracted in Abstracts of English Studies and American Humanities Index.

Journal: Typeset by Fine Line Design (Oakbank, Manitoba, Canada)

ISSN 0092-1912
ISBN 978-0-931362-11-8

Editorial Staff

Editor-in-Chief
Harold Jaffe

Managing Editor
Beverly Price

Associate Editor
Gary Lain

Contributing Editor
Andy Koopmans

Assistant Editors
Ryan Forsythe
Michael Mather
Ryan Kelly

Editorial Assistants
Louie Centanni
Michelle Herold
Conor Higgins
Pat Johnson
Andy O'Clancy
Natalie Quave
Mason Schoen
Shane Roeschlein
Carla Wilson

Front cover image
Ryan Seslow

Front and back cover design
Ryan Forsythe and Norman Conquest

Call for Submissions: Real Time/Virtual

"Virtual" is not just interfacing with "real" time but devouring it—at least in "developed" nations. Half of the world, including Africa, Asia, Latin America, and the elderly everywhere still inhabit real time, but those millions scarcely count. The electronic revolution/devolution seems unstoppable. Who is really profiting from it?

Fiction, non-fiction, indeterminate prose, and visuals which address Real Time/Virtual are welcome. Please submit hard copy from 9/1 to 12/15 2012 to:

Harold Jaffe
Editor, *Fiction International*
Department of English
San Diego State University
5500 Campanile Drive
San Diego, CA 92182–6020

Queries can be emailed to: hjaffe@mail.sdsu.edu

Please allow one to three months for reply or return of submissions. Though we will exercise all due care in handling manuscripts, we cannot be responsible for loss.

Subscriptions

Fiction International is published once yearly.

Annual subscriptions:
Individuals:
$16 plus $2 postage for U.S.
$16 plus $4 postage for international addresses.

Institutions:
If subscription is issued through a subscription service, their terms and rates apply. Otherwise, the rates are:
$32 plus $2 postage for U.S.
$32 plus $4 postage for international addresses.

Some past issues are also for sale. Please see our website (www.fictioninternational.com) or page 128 for a complete list of available past issues and prices. Remember to add applicable postage when ordering.

Use of FI in the Classroom

Please consider assigning this issue (or one of the past issues listed on page 128) as part of your reading list. Ask your bookseller to contact Harold Jaffe (hjaffe@mail.sdsu.edu) for information on availability of multiple copies.

Donating to FI

Although we maintain an office at San Diego State University, *Fiction International* is 100% independent of financial aid from the university. Outside of sales and subscriptions, our continued existence relies on supporters who make cash donations. That is why we are asking people who support the artistic merit of the journal and the progressive political thinking it advances to support *Fiction International* by making a tax-deductible donation.

If you would like to donate to *Fiction International* using a credit card, please visit our website (www.fictioninternational.com) and use the "donate" button to link to our PayPal account. You may also mail a check to:

Fiction International
Department of English
San Diego State University
5500 Campanile Drive
San Diego, CA 92182-6020

Support FI Online

Fiction International maintains an active online presence through its website, blog, Twitter, and Facebook group pages. Please support us by visiting the following addresses and by recommending (friending) us to family and friends.

http://www.fictioninternational.com
http://fictioninternational.wordpress.com
http://www.twitter.com/FictIntl
http://www.facebook.com/FictIntl

Contents

Texts and Art

DISEASES OF THE EYE. 657

1394. **Treatment.** The younger the patient, the more readily will the opacity yield to the treatment. It is sometimes astonishing with what rapidity the part affected is restored in children. The form termed *leucoma* is the most persistent of any, and it may be doubted if medical treatment ever does effect a perfect cure, though time and appropriate medicines may greatly narrow the extent of the opacity. The treatment mostly relied upon at the World's Dispensary consists in enjoining a thorough observance of hygienic regulations and the administration of such internal remedies as the condition of the constitution demands. Prominent among the remedies I prescribe are alteratives and tonics; I also recommend a good and nourishing diet. The absorbents are to be kept continually active by the use of my Golden Medical Discovery. To each bottle add one-half ounce of iodide of potassium. My Purgative Pellets should be used to keep the contents of the bowels in a soluble condition.

Locally, all kinds of stimulating lotions have been employed by experimentalists, and nearly every known remedy has been tried, not even omitting citron-oil and mercurial ointment. To use such agents is unphilosophical and hazardous at any time. Pure sweet-oil, or melted lard, are far superior agents. Various ointments are useful, as fifteen grains of powdered borax in an ounce of lard; or five grains of iodide of potassium in an ounce of lard or fresh butter. The cautious application of diluted tincture of cayenne pepper with a camel's hair pencil, is often useful. More powerful irritants than those already advised, should never be used except by a skillful oculist, for, instead of removing the opacity he may cause destructive inflammation. A lotion of one grain of atropia and an ounce of water applied twice a day, must not be overlooked. When remedies fail, which is sometimes the case in leucoma, or if chalky deposits take place in the cornea, an operation for providing an artificial pupil, illustrated in Fig. 159, may be skillfully performed, and at once restore the vision.

ULCERATION OF THE CORNEA.

1395. Ulceration of the cornea may be caused by purulent, or scrofulous inflammation, injuries, disease of the nerves which

1

668   COMMON SENSE MEDICAL ADVISER.

relieved. Eminent oculists now entertain the idea that in some cases medical treatment is beneficial. Wing says: "There are three conditions presented to the practitioner, viz: first, the cataract may be just commencing; second, it may be almost complete or fully matured without serious complications; or, third, the cataract may be complete or incomplete with serious complications." In the first condition medical treatment may be successful and should consist of a thorough alterative course. My Golden Medical Discovery, with iodide of potassium or the muriate of ammonia, are recommended. In the second and third conditions relief can only be expected by a surgical operation.

1432. The methods of operating may be classified under three general heads, viz: *Division or Absorption, Depression* or *Displacement,* and *Extraction.* By the first method, a needle is passed through the sclerotic (see Fig. 161) and the opaque lens, and its capsule broken into fragments, which by dextrous manipulations are pushed forward into the anterior chamber of the eye (¶ 135), where they are acted upon by the aqueous humor, and dissolved. The pupil, in the figure, appears fully dilated and larger than the cataract, which occupies the centre and is represented by the white spot. This operation is most successful in *soft* cataract, and is accompanied with but little escape of the aqueous humor.

Fig. 161.

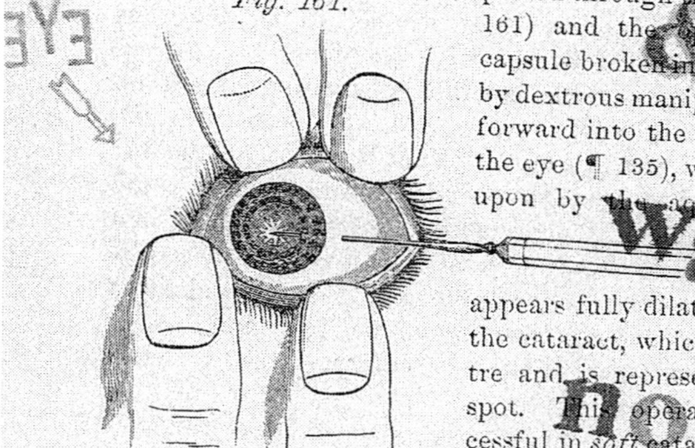

Operation for Cataract, by Division.

1433. By the second method, the needle is passed through the coats of the eye, pushed carefully forward in front of the cataract (the pupil having previously been dilated), and applied to the upper and front part of the lens. It is then pressed downward and backward into the vitreous humor. The needle is retained for a few moments in the eye, until it is ascertained if the lens is disposed to rise; if so, it is again depressed; if not, the needle is withdrawn. This operation is not very successful, as it is liable to be followed by inflammation.

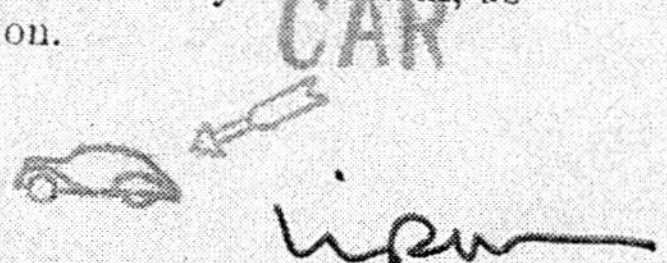

DISEASES OF THE EYE 665

Lesson 2.2

be the result of an exhausted condition of the nervous system, of excessive study, hemorrhage, venereal excesses, masturbation, spermatorrhea, exhaustive diarrhœa, intemperance, cholera, fevers, hysteria, convulsions, sunstroke, derangement of the stomach, suppression of habitual discharges, use of tobacco, etc.

1423. **Symptoms.** The eye is at first weak, which indicates that it must be shaded; it is red and painful, the pupil is dilated and does not readily contract, and there is a mist or blur continually before it. The sight becomes impaired, and there is a sensation as if minute objects were continually passing before the eyes, and one color cannot be distinguished from another. The gait becomes uncertain, and the patient gropes his way along as if in the dark. As the disease progresses the vision becomes more and more impaired, and total blindness is the final result.

DON'T SCREW Up.

1424. Amaurosis is apt to be confounded with glaucoma or cataract. It may be distinguished from glaucoma, which is characterized by hardness of the eyeball and green color of the eye. In amaurosis the pupil is of its natural color, whereas in cataract,

Fig. 160.

HAND

Employment of the Ophthalmoscope.

an opaque body appears behind it. To the person affected with amaurosis objects appear discolored or perverted in shape, and seem to float before the eye; in cataract the vision is clouded but

Lipman

considerably deranged. The iris was contracted, of a muddy color, and effusions of lymph were visible upon it. I advised a strengthening diet, good nursing, alteratives and tonics suited to his case, made local applications to produce dilation of the pupil and allay the inflammation, and protected the eye from the light with a green shade. In two months his general health was much improved, the lymph absorbed, and aside from his eye being a little weak (which sensation was finally removed by an infusion of hydrastin and the use of the Discovery), he was fully restored.

1415. **Case II.** In 1874, George B., aged 20, consulted me for the treatment of iritis, which was rapidly progressing. The iris was of a muddy color, and a peculiar angular deformity existed. I learned upon inquiry that about eight months previous he contracted syphilis and had been treated with mercury and iodine for that disease, but without benefit. I at once commenced treatment for constitutional syphilis. Atropia was applied locally, together with fomentations. At the end of a month there was a decided improvement, and in two months all traces of iritis had vanished, and after further treatment for syphilis, he was completely restored to health.

CLOSURE OF THE PUPIL. (ATRESIA PUPILLARIS.)

1416. Closure of the pupil is characterized by a total loss of sight, and is the result of inflammation of the iris.

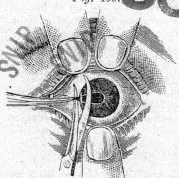

Fig. 159.

Iridectomy.

1417. **Treatment.** If there be any constitutional derangement, it should be rectified by remedies suited to the case. In this disease solutions and lotions applied to the eye are of no benefit, and surgery promises the only relief. If the disease does not extend behind the iris, the surgical operation termed *iridectomy* (Fig. 159) will speedily restore the sight. It is needless to add that such a delicate operation requires a perfect

2   COMMON SENSE MEDICAL ADVISER.

...ich fo... ...resisted ...treatment ...from ...Examination... increased ...es... the conjunctiva, and the blood-vessels were enlarged and tortuous. Several ulcers existed, there was a considerable muco-purulent discharge, and his general health was very much impaired.

Treatment. I directed him to thoroughly observe the rules of hygiene, and gave him suitable alteratives and tonics. The eyes were kept well cleansed, a mild tonic and astringent lotion was applied to them and the ulcers touched once a week with a pencil of sulphate of copper. At the end of one month he had so greatly improved that he was allowed to return to his home in Pennsylvania, and a continuance of the constitutional treatment for a month longer effected a perfect cure. This is but a fair representative of the numerous cases recorded at the Eye Department of the World's Dispensary.

GRANULAR LIDS. (GRANULAR CONJUNCTIVITIS.)

1382. Although this affection is usually spoken of as *granular lids*, yet it generally extends to that part of the conjunctival membrane which covers the globe of the eye, as may be seen by

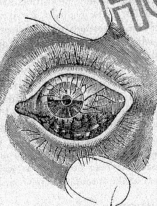

Fig. 157.

reference to Fig. 157. It cannot strictly be considered as a distinct form of conjunctivitis, as it is generally either a result or a concomitant of other forms, and is apt to occur if they be long-continued. The granulations consist of enlarged papillæ projecting from the conjunctiva, and in the milder cases give to the inner surface of the lids a velvety appearance, but in the more aggravated forms a wrinkled, seamed or warty appearance. The disease attacks those generally of broken-down or anæmic constitutions, or whose systems are depraved by previous disease. It prevails to a great extent among the

Granular Conjunctivitis.

Lesson 5.

158. The sclerotic coat (¶ 135) is also sometimes involved. In some cases the pain is intense, in others slight.

Fig. 158.

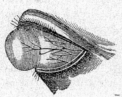

Staphyloma.

1399. Staphyloma may be partial or total. In the first case the projection is comparatively slight, in the second it is very large, frequently rough and uneven and the sight wholly destroyed.

1400. **Causes.** Ulcers, injuries, abscesses and sloughing may all be causes of this affection.

1401. **Treatment.** The treatment must necessarily be chiefly local and consists in a removal of the tumor. If the affection be partial, the operation should be performed as early as possible, for the purpose of arresting its progress and thus preserving the remaining sight. If it be total, the unsightly, morbid growth should be removed, or the sound eye will be quite liable to become sympathetically diseased. Numerous cases have come to my notice in which staphyloma of *one* eye, through sympathy has produced inflammation in the other, and when the tumor, from the diseased eye was removed, the other was restored.

1402. If staphyloma be accompanied by some constitutional affection, those remedies should be employed which are suited to each individual case.

INFLAMMATION OF THE IRIS.* (IRITIS.)

1403. This affection, also known as *Internal Ophthalmia*, may be considered under two forms, viz., *acute* and *chronic*.

1404. The *acute* form does not occur so frequently as the chronic, is more rapid in its course, and when improperly treated, often results in other diseases of the eye, or the chronic form of this affection.

1405. **Symptoms.** There is at first dimness of vision, and the color of the eye is changed; if naturally hazel, it becomes a dark red; if blue or gray, it is changed to a greenish color. The lining membrane of the eyeball and lids has a pinkish appearance. There is a burning, stinging pain, a profusion

* For anatomy of the iris, see ¶ 135.

Lesson 6.

680   COMMON SENSE MEDICAL ADVISER.

1476. **Causes.** The external part of the ear may be inflamed and give rise to this discharge, or the tympanum (eardrum) and adjacent parts may become diseased and suppuration follow. It may be occasioned by injuries, exposures to cold and vicissitudes of climate, or it may be induced by scrofula and translation of eruptions of the skin, or polypus of the ear.

1477. **Symptoms.** There is severe earache, headache, and swelling of the glands of the neck, all of which are symp-

Fig. 169.

EYE

CHAIR

DON·T BE MESSY

Examination of the external ear and tympanum by the speculum and mirror.

toms of inflammation. As soon as the discharge takes place the inflammation subsides. The existence of this disease is very readily determined, but there is oftentimes much difficulty experienced in ascertaining its course and to what extent the tissue

682   COMMON SENSE MEDICAL ADVISER.

in close proximity to the orifice of this canal, encroach upon the passage and necessarily obstruct it.

1482. **Symptoms.** Bubbling, cracking sounds, in the ear, and a disagreeable sensation extending from that organ to the throat. In some cases it is difficult to ascertain the character of the sound, and whether or not the noises are produced by air in the eustachian tube. By use of the Otoscope and Politzer's Air-bag, as illustrated by Fig. 170, the aurist can readily hear the sounds and determine their nature.

Fig. 170.

Examination of the Internal Ear and Eustachian Tube, by the Otoscope and Air-bag.

1483. **Treatment.** If the affection be caused by nasal catarrh or enlargement of the tonsils, the treatment should be similar to that prescribed for these diseases (¶ 878). If the thickening of the tube be so far from the opening that the Catarrh Remedy cannot be made to reach the diseased parts, the eustachian catheter may be used. Alteratives should also be taken, and my Golden Medical Discovery be used.

1484. **Affections of the Tympanum** are all liable to result in thickening or perforation, which may terminate in complete destruction of this organ.

1485. **Causes.** These affections are incident to a scrofulous diathesis, and may result from external violence, as blows or injuries of the head. The tympanum is liable to be ruptured by foreign substances entering the ear, or by concussions of air, as in artillery service. The perforation is more generally due to inflammation or ulceration, the structure giving way to allow the escape of matter, while thickening is usually occasioned by chronic inflammation of the tympanum.

1486. **Symptoms.** Dullness of hearing, giddiness, hissing, puffing, rattling sounds in the ears. By closing the mouth and nostrils, and attempting to expel the air, it will find exit through stance of a few feet from the face. Then alternately covering each eye with the hand, note whether the uncovered eye remains steadily fixed upon the object or has to change its position before it can bring its visual line to bear upon it.—WELLS. There are various other methods employed to discover which is the affected eye.

1446. **Treatment.** If strabismus be produced by disease of the brain, such remedies must be employed as will benefit that affection. If due to an enfeebled condition of the nervous system, tonics, alteratives and nervines should be employed. If to convulsions, antispasmodics (¶ 507) and nervines (¶ 589) are indicated. Some exercise of the crooked eye may be beneficial; for example, shut the well eye and, keeping the head in one position, let the affected member be directed toward a glass and then suddenly open the other. The repetition of this experiment has sometimes been serviceable in restoring the affected eye.

When other means fail, a surgical operation will completely obviate the difficulty. The operation may be performed quickly, and with very little pain. Fig. 165 represents an operation performed on *convergent* cross-eye. It consists in making an incision in the sclerotic, and raising the contracted muscles with a blunt hook, and passing one blade of the scissors beneath the muscles, which are then divided, and the eye is made straight.

Physicians in ordinary practice seldom have occasion to treat these affections, and are therefore not proficient in operating and generally direct the patient to some skillful surgeon. Consequently, at the World's Dispensary there are many cases of this character treated, and I have devoted especial attention to these affections, and am provided with every thing necessary to effect the most approved and successful operations.

29

Fig. 165.

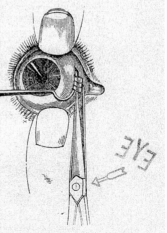
Operation for Cross-Eye.

DISEASES OF THE EYE.

Lesson 2?

BLANK FORM

[a mu]scle which surrounds the eye. Not long since [on an] occasion to [lib]erate up[on a ca]se in which [por]tion[s of] the lids was caused by [c]ontraction of [a w]ound [incl]uding [a] d[ist]inguished surgeon of [N]ew York had removed a [tum]or fro[m] the cheek of th[e] patient, and in healing, [the] skin [has] con[tracted] so much as to result in [the] [eversion] of the low[er lid].

1463. **Treatmen[t].** [If ulcer]is[a]sis be [the cause o]f this affection, appropriate [c]onstitutional [treat]ment is advis[able]. If [cau]sed [b]y contraction of [w]ounds or b[urns,] a surgical [op]eration is t[he] only remedy. The operation [co]nsists in removi[ng] a par[t of t]he tissue, [seen in] the black [lines] in Fig. 167 [whic]h represents the incisions [which] have [been] [ma]de and [turnin]g [the e]dges of the

Fig. *[F]ig. 1[6]*

Ectropium before Operation. | [Ectr]opium immediate[ly af]ter op[er]ation, with the S[ut]ures in position.

[w]o[und] [to]g[ether] and h[o]lding[th]em in position by m[eans of] pins an[d] [silk thr]ea[d] [ap]plied [as presented in] Fig. 168. [If too mu]ch o[f] the superab[undan]t tissue be r[emoved, the op]eration will on[ly] [p]a[rt]ially relieve [the] difficult[y, wh]ile, on [the ot]h[er hand,] too m[uch] b[e t]aken awa[y,] [in]version of the lids wi[ll result. When prop]er[ly] performed, [the] ope[rat]ion is successf[ul and l]e[a]ves little[or no disfigurat[ion].

INVERSION [OF] THE LIDS. [(Entropium.)]

1464. This disease of th[e e]yelid [is e]xactly the [rev]e[rs]e of [the] precedi[ng,] the edge of the [li]d and the [la]shes are t[urn]ed toward the eye. [If this] conditio[n be] continued, [t]he result will [be in]f[lam]mation, caused [by] the irr[itat]ion of the eye[l]ashes, [a]s [described] [u]nder *Wild H[ai]r.*

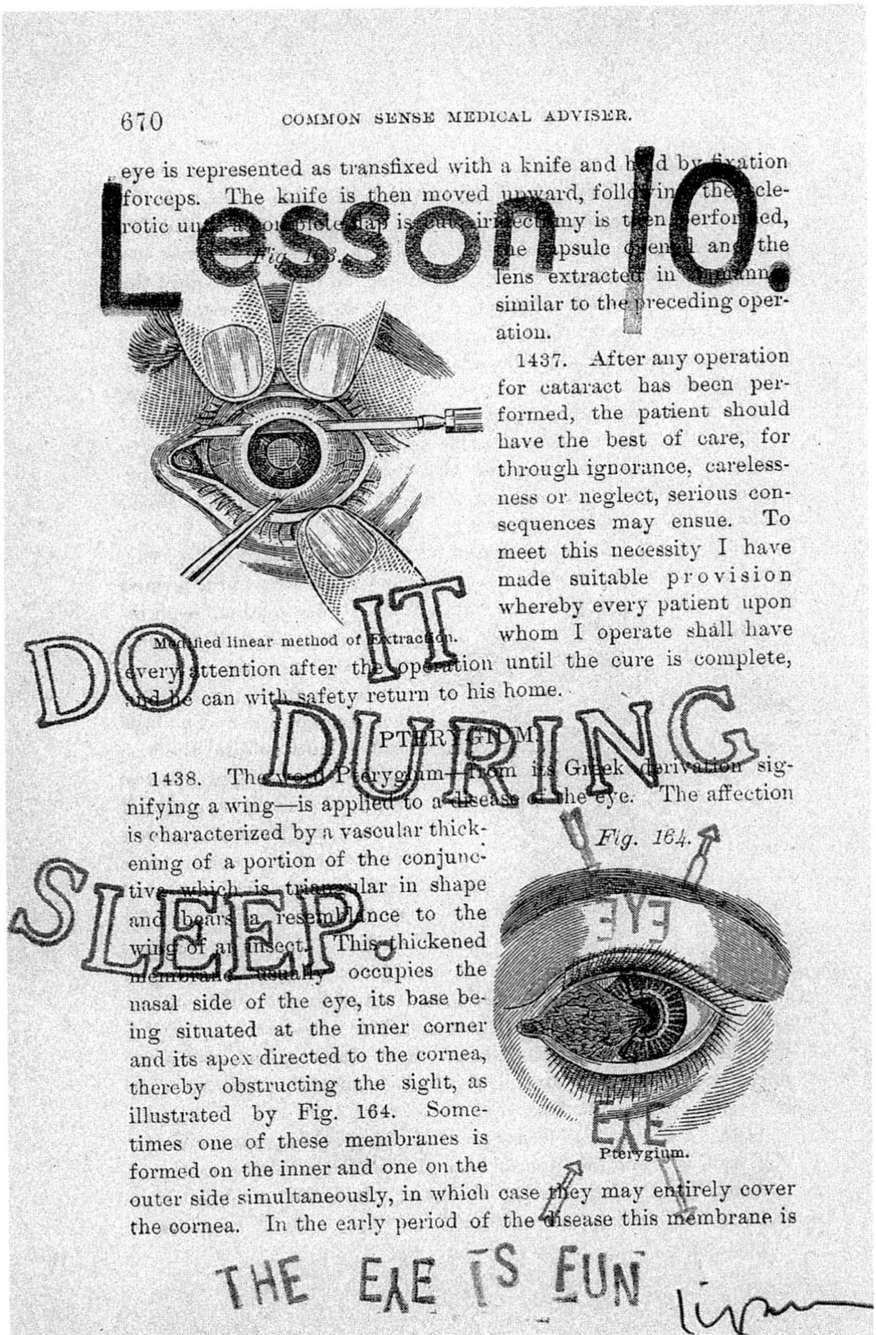

670　　COMMON SENSE MEDICAL ADVISER.

Lesson 10.

eye is represented as transfixed with a knife and held by fixation forceps. The knife is then moved upward, following the sclerotic until a complete flap is cut; iridectomy is then performed, the capsule opened and the lens extracted in a manner similar to the preceding operation.

1437. After any operation for cataract has been performed, the patient should have the best of care, for through ignorance, carelessness or neglect, serious consequences may ensue. To meet this necessity I have made suitable p r o v i s i o n whereby every patient upon whom I operate shall have

Modified linear method of Extraction.

DO IT

every attention after the operation until the cure is complete, and he can with safety return to his home.

PTERYGIUM.

DURING

1438. The word Pterygium—from its Greek derivation signifying a wing—is applied to a disease of the eye. The affection is characterized by a vascular thickening of a portion of the conjunctiva which is triangular in shape and bears a resemblance to the wing of an insect. This thickened membrane usually occupies the nasal side of the eye, its base being situated at the inner corner and its apex directed to the cornea, thereby obstructing the sight, as illustrated by Fig. 164. Sometimes one of these membranes is formed on the inner and one on the

SLEEP.

Fig. 164.

EYE

EYE

Pterygium.

outer side simultaneously, in which case they may entirely cover the cornea. In the early period of the disease this membrane is

THE EYE IS FUN

lipman

Jackson Bliss

When Silence is an Old Warehouse and Love is a Pocketful of Rocks

1

Cubes: It was April and the sun was exfoliating the sky. Before I knew it, I was inside the Art Institute of Chicago with a ticket in my hand. Picasso made more sense than hypothermia.

2

Cylinders: After getting rid of my backpack at the baggage check, I walked up the marble stairs, pushed through the glass doors and entered the Impressionism room. A battalion of ugly teenagers dressed in shorts, baseball caps and sweatpants fiddled with their cell phones, laughing about things they didn't understand. In front of them I noticed a painting of Parisian couples strolling through the city, dressed in serious gray skirts and strict black overcoats, protected by the disenchantment of clunky umbrellas. If there was one flaw this picture had—besides its two-dimensionality—it was the rain. It's impossible to depict rain truthfully because the rain is not a setting, a color or a catharsis. Rain is the mental state you're stuck in when no one sees you as you really are.

3

Spheres: By Chagall's *Praying Jew,* I'd reached my tipping point with haystacks and melting clocks, pig Nazis and Technicolor lily ponds. I turned around and walked past Kandinsky's *Painting with Green Center* to the Cubism room. That's where I saw her for the first time. She was sitting on a bench with her back arched like a Spanish guitar. She could easily have been a college student in her own Blue Period. Wearing pomo glasses, a striped black t-shirt, heather gray cardigan and tight black jeans, she looked young and fashionably malnourished except in the face, where flushed cheeks betrayed the straight lines in her body. Her cheekbones were a bit too pronounced, her lips too luscious and succulent to embody urban starvation.

4

Cubes: I'd never seen such loving sadness before inside a museum. The girl sitting on the bench looked like she was waiting for a reply, oblivious to the whispering security guards in the hallway and the giggling teenagers strolling by in magnetized clusters. I couldn't take my eyes off her: her singular focus was intriguing. Entrancing. For an art student, she was odd and lovely in every way a museum wasn't, and I wanted to understand the world she lived in and the one she ignored.

5

Cones: The next Saturday I returned to the Art Institute and marched straight towards the Cubist room. She was sitting on the same bench, wearing loud red mascara and broken Converse shoes, the corners of her eyes filled with tears shaped like tiny flames of water. Then there was the fruit of her lips, smiling and slightly open, sucking on borrowed air. She was enamored, struck by the same painting: a man (or was it a woman?) with three green noses and two yellow pipes, a checkerboard, and a French newspaper. For an hour I stared at her, and for an hour, she stared at him. Unintentionally we were a reflection of each other, an imitation without awareness. I waited for her to break the silence with a thin little stone, but our moment together was shatterproof. She never looked at me, not even once, to say stop voyeur stop, so I filled my pockets with smooth, polished words I would never throw at her.

6

Spheres: Over the next three months, I returned to the museum every Saturday afternoon. I began to cultivate loyalty and attachment. I felt somehow involved, or at least connected, to the girl in the museum, even if what we shared was a mutual love of distance. It's easier to love strangers because it's their strangeness that stops you from knowing who they are, and it's understanding people that stops you from loving them.

7

Cylinders: The sadness of the girl on the bench disarmed me because her tears weren't an accusation. It's always easier to care for people when you're not the cause of their suffering. And besides, those tears were not a silent violence. They weren't a hormonal plea for chocolate bars or a silent reproach for pointy diction. Her sadness—or mutilated joy, whatever name you preferred—was an old church: a place where tourists congregated to take snapshots of broken history.

8

Cubes: In many ways I felt that I loved her more than I'd loved all my girlfriends of the past. In college, I was an angry child palming fresh hearts with barbed claws. Those girls didn't deserve my selfishness; they were so soft and graceful like tissue paper in gift-wrapped boxes, so easy to rip apart without meaning to. For all those reasons, I loved the girl in the museum. She didn't need me; she didn't protest my existence or demand my affection. She was her own sovereign world and I wasn't part of the victim cartography. And yet, because I was flirting with her dialectically, I wasn't excluded.

9

Cylinders: When I looked at her, I thought of all the words I wanted to say to her, pondering the right way to break our contract of silence. But I oscillated. Sometimes I made up entire conversations in my head, conversations where I always said the right things when I was supposed to, where I was clever and genuine without sounding contrived: Why are you crying? I'd ask. Because I'm alone, she'd explain. But you're surrounded by people, I'd say. Yeah, but I can't see them, she'd say. Well, it doesn't matter, I see you, and your face is getting in the way of the art, I'd say. Is that a line? She'd ask. I'm not smart enough to use formulas, I'd say, but I'm brave enough to threaten your solitude. You're sweet, she'd say. Only in retrospect, I'd say. And then we'd walk outside holding hands, the sun buoying our bodies through the wake of tour groups and street performers.

10

Spheres: Other times, I saw my hand touching the back of her neck. I pictured her turning to me slowly and reciting her feelings: she was a pile of bent silverware and broken pencils, she'd explain, her desire was an aneurysm split into small puzzle pieces of memory, and her words were peeled cubes of fruit, broken apart and siphoned into small units of language that tasted citric and earthy, a hot baritone to my cynical ears. I was the kind of guy that memorized clichés so I could avoid them for the rest of my life. She was the kind of girl that gave you a lemon as a gift and then told you to smell your hands.

11

Cones: She had this way of making stalkers feel original. And I did. I imagined her staring back at me with astonishing scorn; her entire face, disfigured by a broken heart. And it was this fatal fear that prevented me from opening my mouth, except to cough up my dried melancholy. My greatest fear wasn't that she'd berate me but that she'd ignore me completely until I stood up and walked away, ashamed by the porous marrow of love. My silent declaration was a sickness.

12

Spheres: I discovered the pattern of her outfits, a continuum of bold pastels and sharp urban neutrals, conflicting fabric patterns and quiet color coordination. One day, the girl in the museum preferred wearing black high-tops, a light blue military shirt with epaulettes, unbuttoned, and a gray t-shirt with white letters that said *Your Plates are Broken.* The next day, she wore a yellow cardigan with tight sage pants and an orange striped scarf. She combined skin-tight pants with off-the-shoulder blouses, long tube shirts with Puma sneakers and flared hip-huggers, pageboy hats with burgundy hoodies and tweed blazers; 80s-style tank tops with rolled-up jeans and tree-torns. Every Saturday she was an entirely new world, a recreated galaxy of texture and niche, style and Zeitgeist. All of this felt like an expansion of love.

13

Cubes: I had a theory about the girl with a body like a musical instrument. She was redundant, simply art showcasing art, art observing art, art enraptured by art. She was Galatea and Narcissus. She was a work of art reincarnated as a college student. She was motionless, cold and beautiful like the other paintings hanging from invisible hooks. Like all art, she was stuck in time. I could have placed an antique frame around her body and cornered her with velvet ropes, gluing an adjacent title card in midair that said **Transfixed, Anonymous, 2009.**

14

Cubes: Do we love strangers because for one moment we see them as they actually are? Or do we love them because we're allowed to project our own desires and typologies onto them, superimposing our primal template upon their mysterious bodies like film projectors that devise stories out of aluminized screens? Whatever the reason, the point is that human beings love without explanation. The girl in the museum reminded me that I knew how to fall for a complete stranger without knowing who she was, or who she was trying to be. This courage to love came from the inevitability of her separation and the defectiveness of my knowledge. Every time I saw her, it was simultaneously the first and possibly last time we would meet. She was a threat to everything I didn't understand.

15

Spheres: I wanted to understand those celestial trajectories that she weaved out of stardust and orbit lines, painting a new cosmos inside of her grief. She was a self-created theogony after all, a complete and separate galaxy. And somewhere inside this alternative world was a balance of chaos and order, foreignness and archetype, to refresh and recreate you from trampled scriptures. I could have glued an adjacent title card in midair that said **Parallel Multiverse, Anonymous, 2009.**

16

Cones: As summer burned to the end of its incense cone, its ashes turned into strokes of gray stain and autumn down. And as winter became a fortress of ice, shining from the inside like a national treasure of frozen sunlight, I returned every Saturday afternoon to watch her tears falling like broken stars. And like clockwork, like the seasons, like a cut-and-dry integer, she appeared and re-appeared on the bench, more faithful than Pi and more sincere than irony.

17

Cubes: They say that Cubism was a mistake. Cézanne claimed that nature was geometrically divisible into cones and cylinders, cubes and spheres. Braque and Picasso, after a 1907 exhibition commemorating the collective work of the departed Cézanne, took this notion literally. This misunderstanding created a wave of abstract art in 1911 and an illusory love affair in 2009. Seeing reality as it actually is, was not only overrated, but actually ugly too. Truth was less impor-tant than imagination.

18

Cones: She was lonely and found comfort in the multiplicities of art. Her grief was a thin shroud of sadness she wore everywhere she went. It wasn't from drowning in a room of abstract beauty. It wasn't even her chimerical love. What else could it be? Her tears—tiny inverted liquid cones—were the salt of the earth. They expressed collapse and organic rejuvenation, glowing in the eternal light-ness of everything she abandoned. Her translucent tears of glass and silicone were the closest thing to a Cubist homage, using the pastels of her own body to repeat suggestions about perspective.

19

Cubes: It was as if the girl in the museum were waiting for the painting to come to life, to join her on the other side of the canvas where pigments faded, protests turned pastel, and art movements were eradicated by the stormtroopers of theory before their paint could dry. I could have glued an adjacent title card in midair that said **Let's Share the Perishing World Together, Anonymous, 2009.**

20

Cones: Or maybe, within the verb charts of her sadness, she was already creating another world inside her head. Maybe, within the soft folds of her own cognitive dissonance, she and the man with three noses, two pipes and a French newspaper, were in love, holding hands in dual portraits, his hand in one painting, hers in the other; separate paintings hanging beside each other in different easels and sold for 100 francs by a balding Spaniard who lived in a Montparnasse flat.

21

Spheres: I saw her as the Cubists viewed reality: she was art when art was misunderstanding; she was ontological simultaneity, the product of conflict fused together into a unified and irreconcilable field of the imagination. The girl in the museum was a contradiction; she blurred the line between art and artist, painting and portrait, cubism and geometry, subject and object. When I looked at her, I saw every outfit and season, every shape, every constellation and title card. It was easy to love a woman when she was a contradiction: there would always be part of her you would never reach, and part of her you wouldn't understand. Beauty and equivocation, defiance and empathy, strength and separation—these qualities aroused and disturbed me. They were everything that I lacked. Everything I resented. Everything I lusted for in my modern sickness.

22

Cubes: The day I finally broke our vow of silence it was early spring, almost a year since I'd noticed her, and it was raining outside like that large and depressing painting I passed each and every Saturday to observe the girl in the museum, a picture filled with wet couples walking through the desolate streets of Paris in the Impressionism room. Were we—the damned and the disenchanted, the obsessed and the lonely—simply products of sentimental and solipsistic art? Or did we epitomize the flaws of subjective emotion? Where did we belong as flesh and portraiture? On the wall? Sitting patiently on benches? I didn't have the answer to these questions. All I knew was that one April day, I walked up to her and started talking like we were old friends. If I could have glued an adjacent title card in midair to describe the moment, it would have said: **When Silence is an Old Warehouse and Love is a Pocketful of Rocks, 2009.**

23

Cylinders: I'm not sure what I expected, but what I do know is that her voice was incongruous. I thought it would be airy and operatic, or affected and husky; I'd fantasized about this moment for so long that I felt like I was having an out-of-body experience when it actually happened, like a narrative frame within a frame within a frame. The girl in the museum was a small conjugation of time inside my head who an final examination bore no resemblance to the physics of femininity or the formulas of speculation.

24

Cones: In a way you could say she was no longer her own person. She became my own portfolio of grotesque impossibility. If reality were an art critic, it would have objected to my mind: real women have red flesh and blossoming capillaries. It's inhumane to keep my perfect idea (even of a woman), so far away from the oxidation of Real Time.

25

Cubes: In the heavy tome of my daydreams, her voice was high and foreign; she inhaled as she spoke like a Swedish hiccup. In reality, her words were slightly corroded by a Midwest accent and a strong arctic breath that smelled distinctly Wisconsin. She was a pile of discarded frames that deserved to be melted into ash and alphabet. But maybe I just regret the rocks I threw at so many virgin windows, never bothering to find out if there was someone living inside the warehouse.

26

Cylinders: It was an uninspiring opening but my lips trembled. If I could have done it over again I probably would have phrased it differently, or said nothing to her at all, storing my own selfish hypotheses inside the hard–drive of my mind. I had imagined our first conversation in a thousand different ways, but in each version, everything was poetically infected. In my mind, I explained that the concept of art was an incestuous and unstable term. Everything was art, if you wanted it to be, since art has no borders. Nothing was art, if you wanted it to be, since art, by definition, has no definitions. And because art was simply reality appropriated by idiosyncrasy, I'd explain, she was like a man with three noses, two pipes and a French newspaper. In fact, I wanted to tell her, she was more artistic than art because art is always aware of itself, constantly trying to prove something or reflect reality back to the world in a way that feels foreign. But she had no mission, used no mirror, contrived no proof. She was simply a technique, an expression of protean lust and creative love. She was more stable than art. Art was corruption: stained by self-consciousness, borderlessness and aspiration. But she was a perfect idea. She was a portrait of pure emotion and desire that ignored her audience and offered no manifesto.

27

Cones: In my mind, my opening line was supposed to be quirky and thoughtful, but not gimmicky. It would lay the groundwork for countless moments inside cozy black leather booths where we'd make out to sleek Lo-Fi music, our cinnamon-flavored martinis glowing inside the earthy décor of the bistro like broken lava lamps. I pictured us walking up the musty old staircase in my old Lincoln Park apartment, holding hands as summer rain dripped down our legs and left pieces of our insole in every step. I would hold an exhibition inside my bedroom in her honor that went on forever, the snapshots of her life looping into infinity. She would be my one and only flagrant character study. She would be the center of gravity inside the museum and I would be simply a catalogue, a curator who kept the walls clean and the pictures organized, neatly labeled and well-lit. And when the time was right, I would whisper into her ear, slowly and calmly, that she was blurring the line between a painting and its frame, an idea from its creator, a work of art from its exhibition. I wanted to be her one and only critic, her blank-shooting assassin, her corrupted biographer who would tell the story of her story to the world. And even with all that power, I would promise to always love her profile and listen to her voice, storing her permutations inside the catacombs of my memory.

28

Spheres: But that's not what happened. Instead, too much like Marie Antoinette, I said:
—There are a lot of paintings here.
—Sorry? She said.
—I said there are a lot of paintings here.
She shrugged, pulling her cardigan over an exposed shoulder blade.
—I don't pay attention to them.
—Can I ask you a question?
—Shoot.
—Why do you come here?

—Why do you?

—Well, I said, wiping my hands on my pants, I think I'm in love.

—I thought so.

—So what about you?

—I'm in love too.

—With whom?

—With him, she said, pointing to the painting.

—You've in love with a painting?

—You're smarter than you look.

—How does that work?

—Effortlessly.

—I mean, why him?

—Because he's beautiful. Approachable. Faithful.

—But he always looks the same.

—No, he's the opposite of static. He's an amalgam, a series of contradictions, a changing portrait. But more importantly, he's never broken my heart.

—I haven't either.

—But you would, if you could.

—I promise I wouldn't.

—That's just what men do to feel alive. They break things.

—No.

—You've already broken me into a thousand little pieces, to understand me. I can tell by the way you gaze at me.

—The mind can be a beautiful thing too, I insisted.

—The mind is the most violent weapon of all, she said, shaking her head. Instead of trying to understand me, you're assassinating me, cutting my body into a thousand little thumbnails of semiotic porn until I'm nothing except pieces of anatomical confetti, a coronation of your fantasy world.

—But you're not nothing to me, I pleaded. You're so much *more* than that.

—Look buddy, you don't love me. What you love, is a translation. And that's when I swallowed my words and walked away. The rain was inside my head now and the girl in the museum was still hanging on the wall.

Jonathan Baumbach

Breathless Revisited*

Art and theory of art, at one and the same time; beauty and the secret of beauty; cinema and apologia for cinema.

Godard on *Elena et les hommes*

Breathless has aged well. Seventeen years later, Godard's least overtly political film remains his most radical work of art, one of the half dozen signal events in the short history of film. Its imitators—and its influence has been pervasive even among directors who clearly despise its esthetic—have in no way compromised the originality of Godard's first feature. As with most deeply instinctive works, visions not so much of a world as of the art form itself, *Breathless* is essentially inimitable. Audacity is the work's defining impulse. "I wanted," says Godard in an interview, "to give the impression of just finding or experiencing the processes of cinema for the first time." It is not only its freshness and sense of discovery, its breakneck energy and wit that make *Breathless* so exhilarating to watch, but in addition its moment-by-moment defiance of aesthetic injunctions, its thumb of the nose at conventional tyrannies. *Breathless* translates discontinuity into coherence, revises our idea of the possibilities of cinema.

Chance informs the movement of Godard's world (chance and a certain anti-psychology) as instinct seems to be at the heart of his method. The plot, which serves as both parody and metaphoric occasion, is derived from a mélange of American gangster film conventions. In the opening shots, Michel (Belmondo) steals a car, is followed by the police, and, finding himself trapped, takes a gun from the glove compartment and kills the policeman. (We see Michel fire the gun and in a separate shot we see the policeman fall, making it seem as if the firing of the gun and the death of the policeman were only cinematically connected.)

*Originally published in Great Film Directors. Ed. Braudy and Dickstein. Oxford University Press, 1978.

This series of chance conjunctions dooms Michel. Godard assumes the Hollywood code of the thirties and forties in which if a character commits murder, the filmmaker is obliged to murder him in return as a form of symbolic deterrence. The unintentional effect of this code was to predicate the outcome of certain films in advance and to create in the consciousness of the filmgoer a race of doomed anti-heroes and a vision of a mechanically moralistic universe. *Breathless* is the reconstituted fantasy of Godard's filmgoing, and is at once homage to and parody of the America action film and poetic transformation of it.

Breathless, then, is the secret life of the *film noir* (a self-subverting genre itself at its best) made manifest, the film of our filmgoing fantasies. In the American gangster film, we tend to root, despite ourselves, for the survival of the doomed anti-hero, lamenting the mischance that set him wrong. In *Breathless*, the anti-hero, Michel, becomes the rebel we imagine ourselves, a man living his idea of freedom without the compromise of civilized constraint, a figure of ultimate romantic integrity. Humphrey Bogart is his icon. In one of the film's characteristically self-conscious moments, Michel stops to admire a poster of Bogart in *The Harder They Fall* and imagines himself as Bogart, rubbing his thumb across his lips in identification. Michel's self-willed audacity parallels the film's method so that we experience Michel/Belmondo as an agency of Godard, the filmmaker as outlaw, the outlaw as artist. Although romanticized, Michel is never treated sentimentally. He is a character in a fiction. Godard is a dialectician, moving between abstraction at one pole and realism at the other. It is the energy and vision of *Breathless* and not the outcome of its narrative that moves us.

Before *Breathless*, cutting had been used in films for the most part as an invisible seam, a smoothing over of transitions so as to spare us the bumps. The jump-cutting of *Breathless* creates disruption, calls attention to shifts in time and place, to the film as film. By showing us his iconoclastic craft, Godard humanizes the technology of filmmaking. *Breathless* asserts the personality of the filmmaker, who appears in it himself in the ironic role of an informer, betraying his own hero. I can think of no other serious film that lets us get as close to process. Paradoxically, while *Breathless* is an exceptionally naked work, or seemingly naked, it is at the same time mysterious and opaque. Godard gives away the trick of his tricks without undermining the magic of his art.

The film's main disguise is in its narrative which may cause some problems for those viewers (and reviewers) who believe that serious art needs to deal with demonstrably significant themes. Clearly, the hero of *Breathless* is a disaffected punk who breaks the law (who kills) as an emblem of his freedom. Yet we experience him in the context of the film as a vital force, a man inventing his life moment by moment as if he were improvising a movie. The key to Michel's survival is his unequivocal self-interest—integrity is sanity in Godard's world—his seemingly pathological cool.

Love, as the convention goes, undoes him. He moves in with an American girl (Grade B, I am tempted to add), the schizzy Patricia Franchini (Jean Seberg), who sells *Herald Tribunes* on the Champs-Elysées and aspires to be a reporter. Patricia is the self-deceived American bitch-goddess *manquée*. It is the *manquée* that redeems her for us. When she seems most in love with Michel she betrays him to the police—a way, she reports, of testing whether she loves him or not, although more likely it is a repudiation of the demands of love. Michel's death is circumstantial or offers us that appearance. He is tired of running, Michel says, when Patricia tells him that the police are coming. A friend comes by and offers Michel a gun, which he refuses. Nevertheless, as chance has it (or is it that character is fate?), he is shot down, running away, carrying the very gun he refused. Patricia's betrayal, within the film's borrowed conventions, is the killing blow. It is also a fulfillment of character, an act of integrity: a killer kills; a bitch betrays. After his death, in the last shot of the film, Patricia imitates Michel's ritual gesture, rubbing the side of her thumb across her lips, an act of identification. Michel is dead; the rebellious spirit survives. Earlier in the film, Patricia reads the last line of Faulkner's *The Wild Palms* to Michel, "Between grief and nothing I will take grief." Michel is unimpressed. "Grief's a waste of time," he says. "I'd choose nothing. Grief's only a compromise. And you have to have all or nothing." (There are texts in all of Godard's films, literary fragments that coexist with the visual, that parallel and illuminate the action and sometimes merely decorate it.) Throughout *Breathless*, Michel seems to speak as much for Godard as for himself. The character (the icon of Belmondo playing him) embodies the liberating spirit of the film. Godard as critic deplored the impersonality of the well-made French film (what Truffaut called "The Tradition of Quality," the Masterpiece Theater of its day), choosing after a point to refuse discussion of it altogether. *Breathless* is an extension of Godard's criticism, a vision of uncompromising personal cinema, a demonstration of what is possible when a radical idea is carried through to its conclusion.

There are certain unexpected pleasures in *Breathless* that are not often noted in discussions of that work. In contrast to the romance of the gangster plot, the relationship between Michel and Patricia is precisely and realistically observed. Godard takes characters, or prototypes of characters, from Grade B movies and presents them to us with the attention to detail of a realistic novelist. The love story between Michel and Patricia, both self-involved to the point of alienation, is so exactly perceived that it becomes moving and true within the ironic distance of the film's mode.

In almost all of his films—some, of course, more stylized than others—Godard mixes metaphoric action and realistic behavior, creating a world that accommodates both without obvious disparity. The tension in *Breathless* comes out of the attempted synthesis of opposites: cool and hot, intellection and action, documentary and fiction, truth and beauty. There are a number of flawed masterpieces in Godard's prodigious career—*Weekend, Two or Three Things I Know about Her, Peirrot le Fou, Band of Outsiders, Alphaville, Masculine-Feminine, A Married Woman, My Life to Live*—but *Breathless* is his most original and fortuitous achievement, a film in which every miscalculated risk transforms itself into grace gesture.

Norman Simon

The Headache

A woman approaches me in the street. She is not very tall, her hair pale yellow and stiff as straw, her face empty. At her neck, she wears a green scarf. Her left hand presses the side of her head near the temple.

I turn and follow her—she doesn't look back. The streets are crowded. The people are short here—I can see the tops of their heads, rows and rows of them, as if I were looking down from the top of a building. I keep ten paces behind. She is easy to track: her hand keeps going to her head.

The street branches into three and the rows of heads break up. The rightmost fork leads to a museum housing the works of a famous painter. Most go there. The middle branch is the narrowest; an alley, really. I follow the woman down it. After fifty meters she begins to slow her pace and I get closer. She still doesn't turn. I have soft shoes, but I think she hears me. She stops, takes a key out, opens a low wooden door. The medieval houses in this sector have doors in unexpected places, like the orifices of the women in some of the famous artist's paintings. The woman enters easily, but I must make a deep bow. We climb a helical staircase and, at the top, she turns to look down at me, watching as I approach with my head still ducked. On the landing, when I straighten up, I see that I know her. We attended the same secondary school, long ago. I have always been intensely curious about the lives of my former classmates; perhaps this interest is a kind of radar that leads me to them in the streets.

She was pretty as a schoolgirl, but now her mouth is a red lipstick streak, not completely horizontal. There are lines on her forehead, and her cheeks need powdering. *Do you want a girl?* she asks. *You're early.* Her left hand goes to her temple and the lipstick slash contorts and compresses.

No, I don't need a girl. I tell her my name. *You,* she acknowledges. She opens a door. When I follow her through I see that we are indeed in a brothel. There is a red rug and shabby divans where the girls will sit. The light, which comes from shaded lamps, is dim; perhaps the girls do not merit close inspection.

We mount a short flight of carpeted stairs and enter the first door to the left. I must again duck my head. The woman sits on a banquette, her head thrown forward, arms dangling limply between her spread knees. Her stiff hair seems pasted to her head; it hardly moves. I sit on her wide ornate bed, across from her. When she finally lifts her face, I examine it. Her eyes are black points, dabbed below plucked brows. Her nose is fleshy, its lines indistinct. Her hand holds her temple.

Years ago, she was the youngest in our class, and looked even younger, a naïf. Her hair was darker, then. Despite her short stature, she had proportionately long legs and a thin neck. She wore short skirts and showed her legs, a bit of a scandal. She tempted us, but as if from a distance. There was a younger brother who sometimes came to meet her after school. When they stood together, she looked like an innocent child.

While I've been ruminating, she has left the room. Next door there is water running. I am curious to see her nude, but by the time I reach the bathroom she is already in the tub covered by bubbles with only one of her legs sticking out, dangling over the side. *My head is splitting apart,* she says.

I have a vision: A man cleaves a coconut with his axe. The two halves leap into the air, fall and roll, finally stopping far apart.

Water hisses in the pipes, voices float up to us. There must be another bath in the room below. Some of the girls are bathing. How did you get into this trade? I ask. I remember your family was well-to-do. She tosses her head angrily, though her hair remains still. *What does that have to do with it? I was always attracted to the* trade, *as you call it. My father used to attend on Wednesday nights. My mother knew, but pretended he went to political meetings. One night I followed him. I knocked on the door, and the proprietor recognized me and took me to the kitchen. She gave me a Coca Cola to drink, then told me to go home and not come back. I didn't know what kind of establishment it was until a boy at school told me.*

Which boy? She slides her leg further out of the bath and raises it, examining her toes. *Pablo.* Yes, I say, I remember. He was short, but self-contained; he laughed a lot. *I was drawn to the trade,* she tells me. *I would walk by at night, using any excuse. The shades were usually down, but I could sometimes see a woman's face in one of the windows.* The fascists were in power, I remind her. *My father was among them,* she says, *don't you remember?*

I want her to wet her head. Her plastered-down hair looks abnormal, as if someone had ripped patches from her scalp and spread the remaining hairs over the bare places. In fact her whole head seems distorted; the lipstick slash, which ought to have been vertically below the center of her forehead, is instead a few degrees to the side. No doubt, it's her headache that has disrupted her.

Pablo was in love with you, I say. I watched him watching you. She rubs the left side of her head, up and down with her fingertips, seeming not to hear. She turns toward me, but her eyes are closed.

The priests condemned the trade from their pulpits, she tells me, *but their superiors knew it was indispensable for public order.* What did your father think when he found out about you? *What did you think?* she counters. I was not completely surprised, I say. *Pablo was. I was spread out on the bed when he saw me; my breasts were exposed, but I had my legs crossed, hiding my sex.* What did he do? *He gave me this.* She rubs the lipstick slash and red comes off on her fingers. *Let me have a cigarette.*

I put it into her lipstick mouth. It gets wet, but not so much that I can't light it. After she inhales, I remove it, so she can blow the smoke back out. When I put the cigarette in again, she lets it hang from her lower lip, trailing smoke. You could have married, I tell her. I would have married you. *You?* she says. *You were always so far away.*

She takes a last puff, then lets the cigarette fall from her lips to the soapy water. *My head hurts terribly, thank God it's only on one side.* Perhaps the offending side could be chopped out, I think. I ask where the boundary is and she uses her finger to draw a meridian, beginning at her neck, up over her scalp, down her forehead and across the middle of her left eye. I could cleave it with an axe, but then her brain-matter would slide loose. What would that look like?

You must wash your hair now, I tell her. She watches me with her pinpoint eyes, shrugs, picks up the shower spray and turns it on her head. The water splashes up from her scalp, the mist of particles filling the air around her like a halo of light. *Pull the plug,* she orders. The stopper is suspended by a brass chain, now pulled taut. I lift it and, after a moment, the soapy water shudders. Kneeling, I look from the far end of the tub. The surface of the water seems to slope upward, a trick of perspective. I watch her body as the tub slowly drains. Bubbles of soap adhere to her: they are not white, no, rather gray, with bluish interiors; they cover her body like drab blue flowers.

I say: you have never allowed me to see you fully nude. She shrugs. *Others have seen me.* I take the spray and run it vigorously across her, back and forth, until the soap is gone. Her skin looks like polished wood, the pores large, her breasts stark and pointed, the left one slightly higher. Her cunt is a thick black line, moist as fresh ink. She stands and I wrap her in a towel, except for her left arm, which is free to hold her head. Rubbing through the abrasive flesh of the towel, I dry her body. But when I try to remove her hand so as to dry her hair, she resists.

A door leads out from the bath into her dressing room. Shedding the towel, she sits at a dressing table in front of a mirror that stretches the entire length of the wall. I position myself on a stool behind her, watching her reflection. The mirror alters her face. Left and right are interchanged, reversing the asymmetry of the lipstick slash. The black dots of her eyes widen in the glass and there are slight smudges, perhaps in the mirror itself, suggesting eyebrows.

Pablo became a police officer, you know. It made him quite self-assured. He used to come around to my place. It was near the zoo—do you remember? It was before you became a whore, I say. She smiles, the red slash parting. *The apartment was just one large room, but it had a high ceiling and a skylight. The bed was in a corner, under a painting which portrayed a magician and his female assistant. The woman was dark haired, nude to the waist. My bed was hardly large enough for one—I never let Pablo sleep with me.*

Liar!

She turns, holding her head, her face contorted. She is suffering. Her pain is inflicted by God—I am nothing more than a witness. Pablo and I were rivals, I remind her. You gave him one hand and me the other. We went to a cafe together once, the one near the port. You reached across the table to lay your fingers over his, while underneath I felt your leg on mine.

Rub me, she says. Her head feels malleable, as if I could push down to her brain and pull it to the surface in places, forming little convoluted hills which would rise from her scalp. *No, not there.* She takes my hand and moves it to the place where the pain is greatest. My finger touches a little bony knob. *Yes,* she murmurs.

Her head slumps on my chest and I rub for a time, attaining a sensual rhythm. When I raise my eyes to the mirror our images bring to mind the magician and his assistant. Noises come from the floor below, muted laughter. The other whores must be getting ready. After a few minutes, she lifts her head and removes my hand. *Thank you.* I return to my chair behind her, watching in the glass. She unstoppers a bottle, wetting a handkerchief with clear liquid and dabbing at her lipstick. I am afraid that her mouth will vanish altogether, but a thin, horizontal line persists.

Her face looks abnormally pale. She has repainted her lips, getting the lines straight this time, but the color is even redder than before. She powders her cheeks, making them white; she looks like a kabuki performer or a clown. Her wardrobe is open; a clown's costume hangs where I can see it. Put it on, I say. She steps into the leggings, pulling the top up to insert her arms, flinching a bit as the material touches her naked skin. I zip her up in back and close her clown's collar. She stands with her back to the mirror. The broad clown's cuffs extend almost to the floor, her feet bare below them. The costume is checked with large squares of red and white; its baggy contours hide her figure. Above the collar: her white face and red mouth; her hair hanging down, still wet from the bath; her left hand on her temple, fingers spread wide, pressing so hard that her veins stand out in long, ropey lines. THE HEADACHE.

When she removes the costume, her body is flushed; it must have been hot underneath. Her breasts have softened, lost their wooden starkness. Why did you choose Pablo? I ask her. She comes over to me, presses against me. *It was touch and go then, don't you remember? The fascists still might have hung on. Pablo was a churchgoer, a rising star in the police force. My father pressured me.*

More lies. You have always done exactly as you wanted. You joined the trade because it tickled you. Your father must have been wounded terribly. He'd have had you thrown in prison to teach you a lesson, but by then it was too late—the fascists had become impotent. And Pablo? He was a minor official, nothing more. The new government allowed him to stay in office; he might have advanced from there, but he wasn't up to it.

While you became famous, she adds. She is combing her hair now, pulling out the difficult tangles, doubly in pain. We watch each other via the mirror. *You had too much imagination. No woman can survive with that sort of man. Your bizarre visions overwhelmed me. I began to see myself with your eyes.*

You are not suggesting…?

That I finally entered the trade because of you? Admit it, it was your vision of me— a whore.

Only because you behaved like one. It was not only Pablo and I—there were certainly others. When you became pregnant, we might have held a lottery to determine the father.

Her back straightens. In the mirror, the reflection begins to work on its eyes. The brows become darker, the lashes stretch. Mascara is applied. Gradually, the eyes widen, taking over the face. These eyes have seen everything, yet remain solemn and innocent.

Only Pablo loved me, though I didn't love him. He took his place beside me in the church, before God. My father was in his uniform. He stood at attention as I walked down the aisle. You were also there. I saw you in one of the rear pews, sitting alone. You were so tall and thin.

As tall, I say, as Pablo was short. Even you towered over him. Your hair was too long that day, snaking about in all directions. Your fingers stuck out greedily to receive the ring. You made quite a picture, the two of you, standing before the priest—a dwarf and a woman who resembled nothing so much as a tree.

Yes, she replies. *You made it quite clear how you saw us. How cruel you were!* I watch closely as she rouges her cheeks, applies the blush lightly on her forehead, even a touch to her nose. The white, clownlike pallor slowly disappears. Now the finishing touches—she sweeps her hair up, pins it; long earrings pulling at her earlobes; a green necklace. She stands, faces me, posing in front of the mirror. There is a long scar on her abdomen, above the spreading bush of pubic hair. *The fetus went bad in the seventh month,* she explains. *They had to remove it surgically. I was relieved, actually.* She seems to rise from her own hairy bush, a pink stalk, her breasts like fruit, hair a crown of vines. I feel my head begin to throb, the left side. I think I am getting your headache, I tell her. *Poor man!* She touches me briefly, then goes to her wardrobe to dress. A green skirt, tight blouse; nothing under, as befits a whore; finally, soft boots and a hat with a green feather.

I follow her down the red staircase. My footfalls resound through my body, the vibrations in my temple growing stronger. Sounds fly up to us; a bluish tinkle of giggles and chatter. In the sitting room, the whores are lounging on one of the divans. They are in various stages of undress, toilettes incomplete; some sit on the cushion, some on the floor, some lean in from behind. Their limbs intertwine, bodies mingling, a head on a breast, a pair of knees that don't match, red lips blowing kisses. They are like a dense bower of wild flowers, different species, come upon suddenly in the woods. *Half an hour,* she tells them, *then you must get ready.*

I realize I am holding my head, on the left side. The pain is suddenly intense. Surely, she cannot have suffered as much as this. How do you treat your headaches? I ask. She turns to face me, her feather and necklace glowing green. *Nothing does any good. You have to wait—didn't you know that? This can't be your first time?* No, I say, I had them when I was young, but it was years ago. *Won't you choose one of the girls? It might help—at least take your mind off it.*

Where is Pablo? I ask. I should find him, apologize; I had no right to subject him to ridicule. A tear forms in her left eye, dropping suddenly, heavily, like a pellet of translucent steel. *There were two bombs—hadn't you heard? He arrived just after the first, he was first on the scene. Then the second explosion came. It was in every newspaper—how could you not know?* A red blast, brilliant, with fiery edges, body parts scattered on the ground, an arm with a wristwatch, the sky white. I hardly ever looked at the papers, I tell her. I used them to line my floor, to wipe spatters up.

I sit on the bottom step to wait, holding my head with both hands, though only the left side hurts. The pain is terrible—I don't know how long I can stand it. After a time, two of the whores come over. She must have sent them. I can see her at the far end of the room, straightening a picture on the wall. Her green feather glows as if caught in a beam of sunlight. The whores have green eyes, lipstick mouths; they look at me with pity. I know how I must seem to them—my unshaven face black with shadows, my forehead tiny, eyes narrow with suffering; perhaps there is blood dripping from one ear. SELF PORTRAIT WITH HEADACHE. The two whores are rather old, their bodies slack, breasts hanging. Their faces seem familiar; perhaps they are also former classmates of ours, whom she has taken in. Yes, I tell them, I know you. I kiss one and then the other. Why not—while I'm waiting, until the pain goes away?

Charles D. Tarlton

The Turn of Art

A dramatic scene in prose and verse

—for Janet C. Bishop, Curator of Painting and Sculpture, SFMOMA

Gertrude Stein and Alice B. Toklas's *atelier* at 27 rue *de Fleurus, Paris.* It is 1907. The room is filled with heavy furniture, a large writing desk, sideboards, tables, and cupboards.

1. PABLO PICASSO and HENRI MATISSE sit in low chairs across from each other in front of a fireplace. They face us as if looking into a camera (think of the famous photo of Gertrude Stein and Alice B. Toklas by Man Ray taken in 1922).[1]

> On the wall behind PICASSO, 5 MATISSE paintings are hanging— *Woman with a Hat (1905), Madame Matisse (1905), Le Bonheur de Vivre (1905-6), Blue Nude (1907), and Self-portrait (1906).*[2]

> On the wall behind MATISSE, we see 5 PICASSO paintings—*Boy Leading a Horse (1905-6)), Gertrude Stein (1905-6), Young Acrobat on a Ball (1905), Nude with Joined Hands (1906), and Self-portrait (1906).*[3]

PICASSO
once we had turned
our backs on the museums

> *Pause.*

where could we go?

---

[1] The photo can be viewed at http://www.google.com/search?q=27+rue+de+fleurus+man+ray+1922&hl=en&client=firefox-a&hs=PRx&rls=org.mozilla:en-US:official&prmd=ivnso&source=lnms&tbm=isch&ei=DvVkTv2nO6_ZiAKZ6rmqCg&sa=X&oi=mode_link&ct=mode&cd=2&ved=0CAwQ_AUoAQ&biw=1039&bih=568
[2] Matisse's paintings can be viewed at http://en.wikipedia.org/wiki/List_of_works_by_Henri_Matisse
[3] Picasso's paintings can be viewed at http://www.wikipaintings.org/en/pablo-picasso

Indicates MATISSE, sardonically.

then *he* started drawing
lines of paint an inch wide

MATISSE
wasn't easy
while so many others
were portraying

the fine veins of a nose
details in strands of hair

PICASSO
not enough, not
for him, just to make it
look like real fruit

Pause.

no more *trompe-l'œil for him*

Pause.

a dot's enough for a nipple

MATISSE
I drew with brush-
loads of flat blue house-paint

made my lines thick

all around the outside
black between trees and sky

Pause.

MATISSE stands and crosses the room. He takes *Boy Leading a Horse* from the wall and carries it back to his chair. He leans it against the wall beside his chair and sits down.

Not everyone, however, followed my lead.

Pause, admiring PICASSO'S picture.

browns and some grays

this is a precocious child's
drawing. A horse!

a boy's dream of the West
wide open plains to ride

PICASSO
a poetic
dream might more easily
bring in the cash—

hung on their wall till 1913
you often saw it there

Pause, PICASSO points to a spot on the wall

later Nazis forced
von Mendelssohn-Bartholdy
to liquidate
hispano-judaic

art, smuggled out and sold

MATISSE
marketable
like pigeons in St Marks

swarmed around you
as they changed to property

they escaped like wild birds

Pause.

I was waiting
for you to drop it all
come up to art
renounce celebrity

stop showing off—show us!

>*Pause.*

works of genius
make us feel supremely

diminutive

genius has to give it up
forfeit its advantage

PICASSO
has to give up what?

MATISSE
superiority

>*Pause.*

they used to say
I wish I could draw like that

now they say, anyone could

>*Pause.*

PICASSO
I felt deeply
every brush stroke, each of these
as I made them

but in cold aftermath
brought just financial success

>*Pause,* as if reflecting.

I was watching, you know, despite my cool demeanor. But, I loved that life in the cafés, you know, the money, spreading my name around. And the women, they all wanted to touch my genius.

Pause.

You did none of that. You ran no races, gave no quarter.
How was that?

you were ahead
tossing off thick-limbed monsters
driving me mad
you made these obstacles
I had to climb over

MATISSE
Finally!

PICASSO
I wanted paint
with a heavier hand

lose all my fear
of teachers, my father

forget about the saints

MATISSE
could see clearly
down into the world's heart
below surfaces

but you kept painting them,
the surfaces, the smiles

> PICASSO stands and claps. He then crosses the room behind
> MATISSE and removes *Woman with a Hat* and carries it back to his
> chair and holds it on his lap, partly turning it so the audience can see.

PICASSO
this is, of course
all odd lumps of color
unexpected

rub out the woman's face

PICASSO covers the face with his hand.

—and behold Kandinsky!

you sped ahead
on wings of distortion

shape and color
yours to waste, invent

new wonders for the eye

    Pause.

no milliner
could make a hat like that

it was conceived

on an insane palette
laughing, you were laughing

    MATISSE looks around the room, as if trying to orient himself.
    Coughs.

MATISSE
Somewhere near here, art's roadmap changed abruptly. Up ahead or looking just
behind us, out of the corner of my eye, we were poking forward, looking for the
line just so we could step over it. I saw you coming up.

PICASSO
the other side,
how I longed to be free

overstepping
there'd be no looking back

MATISSE
make the first *real* pictures!

2. The stage goes dark. Under a single spot, two middle-aged men emerge from the wings, dressed as GERTRUDE STEIN (PETER CARMODY) and ALICE B. TOKLAS (ANDREW BLIGHT) and wearing the same hats worn in the famous snapshot taken in *Aix-les-Bains, 1927.*[4]

CARMODY (GERTRUDE)
they never knew
what the very next thing

might be—tiny

legs, an arm, both thick as trees
palm tree fronds like fish bones

BLIGHT (ALICE)
They were always searching for it, for the new thing. At first in different ways; Picasso, of course, classically trained, gifted, was a long time shaking off the lessons, his tutored instincts. The Blue and Rose periods—he could have been using a camera.

    Pause.

Henri was different, all for crude outlines, sudden colors, rough dabs of paint, the merest suggestion.

CARMODY
he made it strange
defied the viewer's eye

BLIGHT
no matter what
it was, it disappeared

CARMODY
into paint, just the paint

    Pause.

---

[4] The photo can be viewed at http://fashionhistorian.net/blog/2011/05/12/image-making-gertrude-stein-and-venice-incognito/

That's it, of course. He overthrew the subject.
Only the paint counted.

That was where the eye fell; there, on the paint, the thick paint piling up, the
paint on top of other paint, the paint plowed by the brush like a field readied
for planting.

> *Pause.*

Look on the wall! You see the picture of his wife, *Madame Matisse,* with the green
line down her nose?

See what I mean?

Compare that to Picasso; choose one there on the wall.
What about the portrait of *Gertrude Stein?*

> *Pause.*

...*my* portrait.

> PICASSO and MATISSE rise and retrieve their respective paintings
> and bring them down. They stand under the spot, holding the paint-
> ings in front of their chests.

BLIGHT
He meant it to look like you, a *resemblance,* but he said, if it didn't look like you
right now, that was all right, because it eventually would.

CARMODY
...exactly me.

> PICASSO holds the painting out and turns it so he can see it.

BLIGHT
...or looks like you

he was looking for truth
not just surfaces

behind those eyes, a mind
was watching for a sign

CARMODY
You're right, I had already seen so much. So, I was always waiting, it seemed.

  Pauses, musing.

on the lookout

BLIGHT
your eyes reach out to probe
what you're hearing
as if to say, I had hoped
you'd not be like the rest

CARMODY
And, what do we say about *Madame Matisse's* portrait? Can your discerning eye
probe deeper meaning there? What do you make of that green stripe?

BLIGHT
perhaps he meant
only to encompass
her, register
her contribution to life—
camaraderie in a wife

How could we ever know? No painting means, not in that sense. The planes, the
bumps, the scraggly lines, the lumps of paint, the tiny brush stroke out of place,
lock on the eye, forbid the brain.

CARMODY
I still say it's not just paint; the spirits of all the wild emotions caught up in spread
colors, bone splinters in the *ambergris*—tint, thickness, smell—wide brushes.

It looks like whatever you want it to look like.

  Pause.

BLIGHT
No. It was not about looking, or smelling, or being *like* anything at all.

It meant in fact—red, the green, the violet, and orange; just as it means blue, black, and yellow—in any of their many permutations, in a chance encounter, as crude parts of the world.

Pause.

The flowers ripped from the earth.

Pause. PICASSO and MATISSE come forward and speak.

MATISSE
it was to paint
because I was making

PICASSO
objects from paint

Pause.

my mind's eye gave the world
only the quickest glance

CARMODY and BLIGHT exit.

3. Spot off, stage lights up. MATISSE and PICASSO go back to their chairs. PICASSO points up at his painting, *The Young Acrobat on a Ball.*

MATISSE
there's a story
in that one for certain
pure narrative

focuses attention
on our uncertainty

PICASSO
it was Giotto

or me, could draw perfect
freehand circles

MATISSE
painted like Velázquez
aims now to be a child

> MATISSE crosses the room and stands under his painting, *Le Bonheur de Vivre*. He points up to it.

PICASSO
Childishness, to be sure, yet there's nothing *childish* about it at all. Your hills and distances are but suggested (did you notice?), while the big ideas, all the rest, are wild reds and greens, hints of mythology in all the playful poses; they have only circles and careless dots for eyes, spring frolics, and a touch of sensuousness, perspective out of whack

—verges on the humorous. Far more expressive than my pouting giant or my morose pale hills. Your lovers run in search of cartoon nudity.

MATISSE
So you want to talk about nudes?

> MATISSE reaches up and removes Picasso's *Nude with Joined Hands*. He looks closely at it.

You were still painting like Velázquez.

> *Pause.*

you're so polite
your nude's too well-mannered
covers herself

could be from Pompey's walls
a goddess or priestess

she's a mural
painted on Spanish stucco
inside a church

PICASSO
I meant to make women
of paint someone could love

I was out to show the world who was master. Infinite reflection and dark resignation show on the faces of my men; the deepest sadness, calm, or joy appears on the faces of my women, because they are so beautiful. The children know so much.

I could not paint the kind of pulsing stones, the female boulders you were so happy to make.

    Pause.

I dreamt women
you could take out walking

they'd hold your arm

it took time seeing how
wrong; longer catching up.

4. PICASSO goes behind his chair and takes out a long pointer rod. He goes over to the paintings and stands in front of *Blue Nude*. He points up to it.

    Long Pause. He is just looking at the painting, transfixed for a moment.

this was vulgar
so I at first decided

androgynous
whore-sailor all in one

promiscuously drawn

Pauses again, and leans intimately toward the audience, in confidence. Speaks very slowly.

Porn-o-graph-ic.

Pause, sighs in resignation.

this beautiful hulk is
REALITY

Look at it! Look at it!
hips, ankles, twisted rib cage

Pause, to MATISSE directly, as if, for the moment, giving in.

This was your high–water mark. I knew it instantly. I ran home and drew a hundred chunky naked women leaning on their elbows, sharp hipbones and one leg flung over the other—a hundred, at least.

You had launched a thunderbolt, for certain, but I thought to myself, "I can rise to that, I will rise up to that!"

MATISSE
caught by surprise
lost sight of the way ahead
in a fever to catch up

Pause.

with this the history
of modern art resumes

PICASSO
that we could teach
the art world to embrace
this meaty toad

MATISSE
love and art together
move closer to the truth

PICASSO
The way ahead congealed, the compass and the raw materials were set. Forward!

MATISSE

Indicating the *ateliers*, the walls, the furniture.

If anyone could have seen into the future, this would have been the place...

MATISSE makes an all-inclusive gesture with his waving arm.

...where it all started.

5. PICASSO reaches up and takes down the *Self-portrait* by MATISSE; MATISSE takes down the *Self-portrait* by PICASSO. They both come forward and stand holding the paintings and facing the audience. PICASSO pulls a false beard from the portrait of MATISSE. The two portraits reveal a strong family resemblance—the portraits of two brothers.

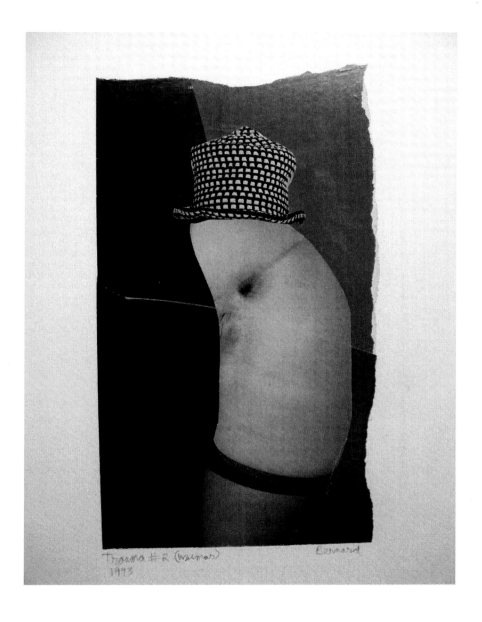

Gerald J. Butler

A New Way of Seeing: The Night Sky of the Enlightenment, William Herschel's Disposition Toward the Empirical, and 'Profundity'*

In the introduction to her recent study, *Science in the Age of Sensibility,* Jessica Riskin emphasizes that the "hardnosed, unemotional reputation" that empiricism came to have, as embodied in Dickens' nineteenth-century caricature, Thomas Gradgrind, was not at all how scientific empiricism was perceived a century before "to the philosophes who received the young doctrine from its seventeenth-century progenitors [...]. To them, empirical knowledge was not a matter of impassive adherence to the hard facts of sensory experience, but rather one of sensibility."[1] Professor Riskin makes a strong case that in a cultural milieu where Richardson and Sterne were for Diderot favorite novelists (Riskin, 8), their emphasis on feeling, promoted by eighteenth-century literature, interpenetrated scientific method itself. By the same token, it would make sense to look at eighteenth-century science in terms of literary history, even a history of genres. Here I would like to consider Sir William Herschel's astronomical researches as a way of *reading* and suggest that the empiricist cast of his mind can be understood as his ability to read the night sky as if it were written in the new genre of the novel rather than as a kind of poetry.

---

[1] Jessica Riskin, *Science in the Age of Sensibility: The Sentimental Empiricists of the French Enlightenment* (Chicago and London: University of Chicago Press, 2002) 1. It is understandable that she wishes to insist that eighteenth-century French empiricists valued feeling and that this had significant political and economic implications; she coins the phrase "sentimental empiricists" to identify them. It seems to me there may be a problem in using the word "sentimental" this way because the term has a critical sense that according to the *Oxford English Dictionary* was already in use by the time of Sterne. Thus, calling them "sentimental empiricists" might sanction a devaluation of empiricism from, as it were, the opposite direction than that represented in the Gradgrind character.

1.

The achievement of Herschel may be underestimated for other reasons than the devaluation of empiricism given in the figure of Gradgrind. Thus, in a twentieth-century popularizing book on astronomy, Sir James Jeans describes the discovery of Uranus in this way: "Sir William Herschel discovered Uranus quite accidentally in 1781, while looking through his telescope with no motive other than the hope of finding something interesting in the sky. By contrast, Neptune was discovered in 1846 as a result of intricate mathematical calculations, which many at the time regarded as the greatest triumph of the human mind, at any rate since the time of Newton."[2] Herschel's own words are a good reply to this dismissive view. "It has generally been supposed that it was a lucky accident that brought this star [i.e., the planet Uranus] to my view; this is an evident mistake. In the regular manner I examined every star in the heavens, not only of that magnitude but of many inferior; it was that night *its turn* to be discovered. I had gradually perused the great Volume of the Author of Nature and was now come to the page which contained a seventh Planet. Had business prevented me that evening, I must have found it the next, and the goodness of my telescope was such that I perceived its planetary disc as soon as I looked at it; and by application of my micrometer, determined its motion in a few hours."[3]

As a matter of fact, Herschel was not the first to discover Uranus in the sense of merely seeing it. "The earliest records of Uranus are by Flamsteed in 1690 (he called it a star, 34 Tauri), 1712 and four times in 1715. There were at least 15 other sightings by three other astronomers before Herschel's discovery."[4] Indeed, under good conditions Uranus can actually be seen by the naked eye.[5] Its planetary motion over the centuries could well have been evident. Herschel detected that motion "in a few hours" by means of his micrometer, but surely Flamsteed between 1690 and 1715 could have detected the motion had he thought to notice it. The discovery of Uranus as a member of the solar system was the result of careful observation and measurement by a mind prepared to see what was not *supposed* to be there.

Actually, as Agnes M. Clerke put it in 1895, a "'review of the heavens' was a complete novelty."[6] Furthermore, Herschel made his careful "reviews" of the night sky because he was deeply interested in a part of astronomy that, ironically,

---

[2] Sir James Jeans, *The Universe Around Us* (New York: Macmillan, 1931) 18.
[3] Constance A. Lubbock, editor, *The Herschel Chronicle: The Life-Story of William Herschel and his Sister Caroline Herschel* (Cambridge, England: Cambridge University Press) 78-79.
[4] "Uranus," Royal Observatory Greenwich and National Maritime Museum, http://www.rog.nmm.ac.uk/leaflets/solar_system/section3.12.html.
[5] In August 2002, for instance, *Sky and Telescope* told its amateur readers that "Uranus is just bright enough to glimpse with the naked eye when it can be viewed high up in truly dark skies. This 5.7 magnitude planet appears 3.7" across [...] at this opposition [...]. *Sky and Telescope* (August 2002) 101-102.
[6] Agnes M. Clerke, *The Herschels and Modern Astronomy* (New York: Macmillan, 1895) 19.

had for some time ceased to be of much interest to astronomers: the stars themselves. It was the *planets* that mattered to Herschel's contemporaries, because repeated observation of their orbits constituted a test of the Newtonian system and because planets could be magnified to discs on which surface features could be seen. The much more distant stars remained points no matter how high their magnification; the stars were regarded as mere reference points against which to trace the motions of the planets.[7] While astronomers by the eighteenth century had generally come to accept the Copernican system, when it came to the stars themselves it was as if the old earth-centered system still held sway over their imaginations. Even Aristotle had realized that the observation that Venus and Mercury change in brightness indicates that their distance to the earth changes, but he nevertheless held to the conception of earth-centered concentric spheres.[8]

2.

"Hitherto the sidereal heavens have, not inadequately for the purpose designed, been represented as the concave surface of a sphere," Herschel wrote, "in the center of which the eye of an observer might be supposed to be placed." But Herschel broke out of this emotionally-satisfying mythopoetic view. "The construction of the heavens," he continued, "in which the real place of every celestial object is to be determined, can only be delineated with precision when we have the situation of each heavenly body assigned in three dimensions, which in the case of the visible universe may be called length, breadth, and depth; or longitude, latitude, and Profundity."[9] It is this dimension of "Profundity" that, according to Herschel, continued to be excluded from the considerations of astronomers long after Aristotle and even Copernicus and Galileo.

Thus, according to the historian John North, "when Huygens in 1656 in looking through a telescope found the famous nebula in Orion, the area of sky around it was so black that he thought he was looking through a hole in the heavens into the luminous regions beyond" and William Derham in the eighteenth century could still maintain "that stars may be openings in the heavens to a brighter region beyond."[10] The earth-centered conception of the "sidereal heavens" still keeps them separated in imagination from the earth, seen as the sink to which all that is material must fall, while all that is spiritual, lofty, pure is freed from gross materiality and can ascend heavenward. The emotional pain of letting

---

[7] Clerke 17-19. Also Richard Panek, *Seeing and Believing: How the Telescope Opened Our Eyes and Minds to the Heavens* (New York: Penguin, 1998) 112-13.
[8] See Gerald E. Tauber, *Man's View of the Universe* (New York: Crown Publishers, 1979) 47. "Aristole," John North maintains, "has, then, a heaven that is in sharp contrast with the sublunary world of change and decay. It is unique, ungenerated and eternal—qualities that will present Christian Aristotelian apologists with problems" (*The Norton History of Astronomy and Cosmology* [New York and London: W. W. Norton, 1995] 82).
[9] See Panek 106.
[10] North 402-403.

go of the earth-centered conception in response to empirical evidence, as well as to Cartesian doubting, was already expressed in 1611 by John Donne in his *An Anatomy of the World:*

> And new Philosophy cals all in doubt:
> The Element of fire is quite put out;
> The Sunne is lost, and th'earth, and no mans wit
> Can well direct him, where to looke for it.
> And freely men confesse, that this world's spent,
> When in the Planets, and the Firmament
> They seeke so many new [...]. (lines 205-11)[11]

According to Donne, this "doubt" parallels disruption in all social relationships. The impact of empirical evidence has been to upset the metaphors and analogies—poetic devices—which heretofore served to model the moral and physical universe. Donne represents these fatal disruptions in figures of speech as the death of a "she" who is a feminine principle now eliminated from the world, and his anxieties show how difficult it is for the imagination to free itself from an earth-centered conception of the cosmos. Indeed, even though the earth-centered system had been *intellectually* questioned by astronomers by the time *Paradise Lost* was published,[12] Milton's angel Raphael warns Adam that, while the truth may in fact be otherwise, "To thee who has thy dwelling here on earth" the earth-centered view should suffice.[13]

Besides the fact that earth-centered views provide appropriate metaphors and analogies for traditional theological/social beliefs, they are easy to visualize and lend themselves to being made into small models. According to North, an actually existing small model may have been in Plato's mind when he conceived the myth of Er for the tenth book of *The Republic* (North 69). Such small models even in conception exhibit most if not all of the qualities of beauty set forth in Burke's 1756 *Enquiry*—smallness, smoothness, variety in the direction of the parts, nothing angular in those parts, delicate formation, and clear, bright coloration without any glaring color unless "diversified with others."[14]

---

[11] John Donne, *The Anniversaries,* ed. Frank Manley (Baltimore: Johns Hopkins Press, 1963) 73.
[12] Issac Asimov, *Asimov's Annotated* Paradise Lost (Garden City, New York: Doubleday, 1974) 10 note 20. "Some astronomers," Asimov says, "even two centuries before Milton, had speculated that the stars were other suns, equal to and in some cases superior to our own, and appearing as sparks only through their great distance. [But i]n the Miltonic universe, earth-centered, no such speculation could find a place" (332 note 472).
[13] The admonition concerning cosmological curiosity is in Book VIII, lines 65-177. (John Milton, *Complete Poems and Major Prose,* ed. Merritt Y. Hughes [New York: Odyssey Press, 1957] 364-7.)
[14] Edmund Burke, *A Philosophical Enquiry into the Origins of our Ideas of the Sublime and Beautiful,* ed. J. T. Boulton (London: Routledge and Kegan Paul, 1958) 117.

In Burke's terms, these models would make the cosmos into something *love-able*—a place, as it were, for which Adam can be grateful. But Herschel's conception of the third dimension of the night sky eliminates the possibility of a small, beautiful model. In his paper of 1783 on the proper motion of the sun he argued that the solar system itself is moving towards a point in the constellation Hercules (λ Herculis), a view that (according to modern measurements) M. A. Hoskin says "is not far from the truth" and "a well-judged conclusion drawn from the minimum of data by straightforward inspection" available to him.[15] Such motion is hardly visualizable at all, especially when we consider that the so-called "fixed stars" in Hercules themselves have proper motions. Furthermore, Herschel knew that light itself has a finite speed, which had been measured to within an accuracy of one percent by 1728, so that what we see does not tell us where these distant stars are but where they *were* some time in the past.[16]

By the beginning of the eighteenth century, astronomers generally imagined a heliocentric but infinite universe.[17] But if poetry finally would have to abandon the earth-centered cosmos, it had other resources. In the mid-eighteenth century James Thompson imagined a Newton who "wanders through those endless worlds" and the sky as a "blue infinite."[18] In Burke's terms, Thompson's infinite universe is sublime.[19] But Herschel aspired to find, by means of larger and larger reflectors, the *end* of the universe, at least as that meant the Milky Way galaxy. The amount of light a telescope can grasp is a function of the aperture of its objective—in other words, main lens or mirror—and it is light-grasp Herschel needed to be able to glimpse fainter and fainter objects. Thus his choice to build reflectors rather than refractors.

The long-focus refractors with small apertures to minimize optical aberrations were required for the repeated observation of planetary orbits and the magnification of planetary discs, but the reflector, whose single surface was not capable of the amount of correction of the refractor, could nevertheless be made relatively easily with a much wider aperture than any refractor could (Panek 112-30). Still, he could not build big enough reflectors because the speculum metal out of which the mirrors then had to be made sagged under their own weight and introduced too much distortion. And so he had to give up fathoming "Profundity"; it would take the instruments we have today to determine the end he sought.[20]

[15] M. A. Hoskin, *William Herschel and the Construction of the Heavens* (London: Oldbourne, 1963) 54.
[16] Michael Fowler, "The Speed of Light," http//galileoandeinstein.physics.virginia.edu/lectures/spedlite.html
[17] Peter Hans Reill and Ellen Judy Wilson, *Encyclopedia of the Enlightenment* (New York: Facts on File, 1996) 94.
[18] "To the Memory of Sir Issac Newton," in *English Poetry of the Restoration and Early Eighteenth Century,* ed. H. T. Swedenberg, Jr. (New York: Alfred A. Knopf, 1968) 427-32.
[19] As Burke tells us, "hardly anything can strike the mind with its greatness, which does not make some sort of approach to infinity" (63).

But his empirical temperament rejected poetry outright. As a young man first coming to England, Herschel had a strong interest in Locke's *An Essay Concerning Human Understanding* and must have read with approval the famous passage in Book II, Chapter XI.2 criticizing "metaphor and allusion."[20] Years after his encounter with Locke, when Dr. Burney read to him Book VIII of his twelve book "Astronomy, an historical & didactic Poem,"[22] Burney recorded that Herschel told him "'he had never been fond of Poetry—He thought it to consist of the arrangement of fine words, without meaning [...]." Admittedly, according to Burney Herschel added "but when it contained science and information, such as mine (hide my blushes!) he liked it very well" (Lonsdale 390). Nevertheless, Burney's biographer Roger Lonsdale concludes that "there is no evidence to know what Herschel really thought of his poem" (390) and even suggests that on one occasion Herschel may have tried to avoid hearing more of it (397).[23] "Science" or "information" conveyed in a poem might make it interesting to Herschel, but he had little interest in ancient astronomers who, it appears, were much the subject of Burney's poem—not even if their work was presented in an historical pageant of which he himself was the hero.

What limited his empirical disposition was not a need for poetry but, according to Hoskin, his "quality of perseverance that could so easily degenerate into sheer obstinacy" because, "coming to astronomy in middle age"l he worked at his projects "as though he had few tomorrows" (190). For all his respect for observation he could stubbornly cling to an erroneous conception. Thus he was wrong to correlate the distance of the object to its apparent dimness with the kind of

---

[20] The end of the universe is about 14.5 billion light years away—looking out in any direction from any point for the end—its beginning. Beyond that, the cosmic microwave background radiation is impenetrable to optical telescopes but itself reveals by space observation at radio wavelengths features of the "Big Bang" itself.

[21] "For wit lying most in the assemblage of ideas, and putting those together with quickness and variety, wherein can be found any resemblance or congruity, thereby to make up pleasant pictures and agreeable visions in the fancy; judgment, on the contrary, lies quite on the other side, in separating carefully, one from another, ideas wherein can be found the least difference, thereby to avoid being misled by similitude, and by affinity to take one thing for another. This is a way of proceeding quite contrary to metaphor and allusion; wherein for the most part lies that entertainment and pleasantry of wit, which strikes so lively on the fancy, and therefore is so acceptable to all people, because its beauty appears at first sight, and there is required no labor of thought to examine what truth or reason there is in it. The mind, without looking any further, rests satisfied with the agreeableness of the picture and the gaiety of the fancy. And it is a kind of affront to go about to examine it, by the severe rules of truth and good reason; whereby it appears that it consists in something that is not perfectly conformable to them" (John Locke, *An Essay Concerning Human Understanding,* ed. P. H. Nidditch [Oxford: Oxford University Press, 1975] 156-57).

[22] See Roger Lonsdale, *Dr. Charles Burney: A Literary Biography* (Oxford: Clarendon Press, 1965) 385. Finally, the effect of remarks about his "crabbed chapters" about "paralaxes" by Lady Crewe made him realize, Lonsdale claims, "that for years he had been boring his friends in the belief he had been entertaining them"—a realization that may be "sufficient to explain the fate of his poem" (404).

[23] Ultimately, Burney destroyed the manuscript. Some fragments of the poem do remain, and Scholes, Burney's earlier biographer, provides us with four lines:
Great Newton's comprehensive soul
Saw system after system rowl.
Could read the rules, explain the Cause
Which kept them from the given Laws.
Scholes provides us with a critical comment as well: "From this sample it would appear that though we may have lost a clear and succinct exposition of the history of Astronomy we have not lost great poetry" (Percy A. Scholes, *The Great Dr. Burney: His Life—His Travels—His Works—His Family and his Friends,* [London: Oxford University Press, 1948] 157).

accuracy in each particular case that, for instance, guided his interest in double stars. When viewed with a telescope, many of the stars in our galaxy appear double or in even greater multiples, and Herschel wanted to see the doubling as a coincidence so that the dimmer of the pair would then be further away than the brighter and he could attribute any apparent motion between them to parallax which he could measure and so calculate the stellar distances. For a long time he would not admit the evidence that the members of these systems were close to each other because gravitationally bound. Nevertheless, he finally did accept the evidence to the contrary of his strongly-held belief. Perhaps even inordinate ambition, along with a tendency to over-theorize, gets less in the way of accepting empirical data than does the need for poetry.

3.

If Herschel's empiricist temperament entails a rejection of the poetic, including both the beautiful and the sublime, and even an outright dislike of poetry, novels were another matter for him. "Generally I was obliged to read to him at those times whilst he was at the turning lathe or polishing mirrors," his sister Caroline tells us, "*Don Quixote, Arabian Nights Entertainment,* the novels of Sterne, Fielding, etc...."[24] Herschel's disposition for the empirical would be especially congenial to the realism of the novel conceived as in dynamic opposition to cultural ideals embedded in myth and poetry.

This dynamic is often commented on in the eighteenth century. In his famous complaint in *Rambler* 4 (March 31, 1750), Johnson points out the danger to the morals of young people of the kind of fiction that tries accurately but indiscriminately "to imitate nature."[25] If we applied Johnson's caution concerning realistic fiction to astronomical research, we should say if we cannot restrict ourselves to evidence that can be made to support the earth-centered cosmology—since such a cosmology provides the metaphors that help to reinforce the moral universe Donne saw crumbling—we should admit nothing that would exclude the sublime, for the sublime can induce awe for "creation." Admittedly, the presence of the *Arabian Nights' Entertainments* on his sister's abbreviated list would seem not to fit with a preference for novels whose force, even in the case of *Tristram Shandy*

[24] Helen Ashoton and Katherine Davies. *I Had a Sister: A Study of Mary Lamb, Dorothy Wordsworth, Caroline Herschel, Cassandra Austen* (1937. Folcroft, Pa.: Folcroft Library Editions, 1975) 178-89.
[25] "It is justly considered as the greatest excellency of art to imitate nature; but it is necessary to distinguish those parts of nature which are most proper for imitation: greater care is still required in representing life, which is so often discoloured by passion, or deformed by wickedness. If the world be promiscuously described, I cannot see of what use it can be to read the account; or why it may not be as safe to turn the eye immediately upon mankind, as upon a mirror which shows all that presents itself without discrimination. It is therefore not sufficient vindication of a character that it is drawn as it appears, for many characters ought never to be drawn; nor of a narrative that the train of events is agreeable to observation and experience, for that observation which is called knowledge of the world will be found much more frequently to make men cunning than good. [...]."(*Samuel Johnson,* ed. Donald Greene [Oxford: Oxford University Press, 1984] 177).

(where, as Melvin New points out, the "Shandy dreams wreak themselves" against physical reality[26]) depends on their subversion of cultural myths. But we might suppose the interest for him in the Arabian Nights would lie in the very "orientalism" that could function to oppose myths familiar to him, as merely European romances, rehearsing those myths, cannot (without self-parody) easily do.[27]

It would seem that there has been a paradigmatic shift in thinking since the eighteenth century that now *welcomes* the shock of the new and even sees the subversion of what is culturally accepted as the essential purpose of the literary. Even so, we can hear Johnsonian anxieties in Robert C. Holub's warning us of the dangers in the contemporary "reception theory" of Jauss and Iser which is indebted to the concept of "defamiliarization" that values the "breaking of horizons of expectation." "But if Iser," Holub writes, "indeed insists that literature 'takes its selected objects out of their pragmatic contexts and so shatters their original frame of reference' […] he too falls victim to what Jauss has labeled the aesthetics of negativity […]. For this reason his theory displays the characteristic difficulty in accounting for the 'affirmative' literature of the Middle Ages, and he is ultimately compelled to regard the greater part of this tradition as 'trivial.'[28]

But the myths held dear in the Middle Ages, and long before, whether they are about cosmology or the human relations that cosmology is produced by and reproduces, need not be held dear by us. "The novel," wrote D. H. Lawrence, "is a great discovery: far greater than Galileo's telescope or somebody else's wireless."[29] Leaving aside which is the greater achievement, novel or telescope, we may observe that both can function as instruments of enlightenment. The telescope in its modern form, and as instrument for capturing electromagnetic energy outside the optical spectrum, has led to an increasingly deep understanding of physical nature. But Hume maintained that "all sciences have a relation, greater or less, to human nature,"[30] and it is the novel that puts forth the claim to an understanding of that nature—the only item on the "Bill of Fare" offered at the beginning of *Tom Jones*. In using either telescope or novel to make observations that require a sensitivity not present in the caricature of empiricist as Gradgrind, we may have to give up the pleasures of beauty and sublimity, but we may gain instead, to use Herschel's word, "profundity."

---

[26] Melvin New, *Laurence Sterne as Satirist: A Reading of* Tristram Shandy (Gainesville: University of Florida Press, 1969) 202-203.
[27] "Although the taste for such 'moorish' and oriental narratives was quickly derided by some as a fanciful and romantic waste of time suitable only for supposedly weak-minded women and children, it soon became clear that the *Nights* was destined to become one of the most widely read and influential collections of stories ever to be published in English. Swift, Pope, Johnson, Walpole, Gray, Goldsmith, and Gibbon were to be counted among the collection's earliest admirers; the nineteenth century would trace the influence of the *Nights* in the works of novelists such as Scott, Austen, Thackeray, Dickens, and Charlotte Brontë" (The *Arabian Nights' Enterainments*, ed. Robert L. Mack [Oxford: Oxford University Press, 1995], prefatory note).
[28] Robert C. Holub, *Reception Theory: A Critical Introduction* (London and New York: Routledge, 1982) 87.
[29] D. H. Lawrence, "Reflections on the Death of a Porcupine," in *Phoenix II: Uncollected, Unpublished, and Other Prose Works by D. H. Lawrence*, ed. Warren Roberts and Harry T. Moore (New York: Viking Press 1970) 416.
[30] David Hume, *A Treatise of Human Nature*, ed. David Fate Norton and Mary J. Norton (Oxford: Oxford University Press, 2000) 4.

*

Under a somewhat different title, this was originally presented as a *communication* to a colloquium at the University of Paris-III and included in *The Enlightenment by Night: Essays on After-Dark Culture in the Long Eighteenth Century,* ed. Serge Soupel, Kevin L. Cope, and Alexander Pettit [New York: AMS Press, 2010], a collection of the *acta* of the colloquium.

Mark Wallace

from **We Need to Talk**

Condoleeza Rice is saying the U.S. doesn't guarantee security for Iraq.

Movie critics are saying *The Da Vinci Code* film is no good, although box office sales say large numbers of people are going. A *Los Angeles Times* editorial says people are going because in America, belief is purchased like any other product, and Americans no longer feel accountable to anyone else about what they believe. In this environment, the editorial says, the idea of evidence becomes irrelevant.

The Wall Street Journal says some business leaders are saying that in the age of the Blackberry, it no longer matters where CEOs spend their work time.

Lorraine and I talk about whether it's raining too hard for me to walk to the train. We talk about how people say it never rains in San Diego when in fact it rains a lot. We talk about whether I've packed everything. It seems I have, but I say I never feel like I have.

The National Weather Service says that there will be occasional rain in San Diego this week but that in DC, the whole week will be sunny.

Dan and Mike are telling each other shit stories over email, and ranking their favorites.

On the Rocktown email list, people are talking about the importance of a Look for rock bands and what the difference is between a Look and a Uniform.

On the Now What blog, novelist Jeffrey DeShell says that language poetry theory is an oxymoron. He says that writing a novel is hard, and that he's never found a writer who's good at writing both novels and poetry.

In the airport terminal, a little girl says, "Look how strong I am," and lifts a full bookbag as big as she is.

A man sitting behind me in the airport says, "We were driving more than a hundred miles an hour. If we were abducted, we don't remember it."

The airport intercom says, "Do not leave your baggage alone at any time. If you believe your baggage has been tampered with, or if someone asks you to carry a foreign object, please report it to airport security immediately. Remember, security is everyone's responsibility."

The cab driver from National Airport in DC asks me what life's like in San Diego. I tell him it's expensive and everyone has to drive a lot. He says he's finding it harder to live in Washington, where the weather gets both very cold and very hot. I tell him that a lot of people in Washington tell me the same thing and that the San Diego area is crowded. He asks what the weather was like when I left San Diego, and I tell him oh, about like what it is here tonight, in the sixties and drizzling. "Only like this?" he says, disappointed. "What's life like in San Francisco?"

I finally get to Tom's apartment, where I'm staying, and I tell him about the plane ride, how the air conditioning wasn't working right and the plane kept going from too hot to too cold. Meanwhile, I said, there was turbulence most of the way so for almost five hours the plane was shaking while the temperature kept fluctuating wildly. It almost made me sick, I said. The story seems a good one and I tell it a number of times before my trip is over.

Tom and I had last talked at the Postmoot Festival at Miami of Ohio University about a month earlier, and now we were talking in DC, and next month Tom is planning to visit me and others out in southern California and we'll do some talking there. "So we're having a party on both coasts party," I say. Tom says we're actually having the party on three coasts.

The next afternoon, at her apartment, Maryn tells me she's been reading the Craigslist casual encounters section. She says, "Mostly it's men sending in pictures of their dicks." She says almost no women write in, that even the posts that seem to be from women are usually from men or sometimes maybe from prostitutes. Maryn tells me that one night before bed she wrote in: "In ten minutes I'm going to masturbate and go to sleep," and then added, "Send me your best sex stories and maybe I'll ask you to come over. I want them to be well written." She says that within an hour, she had about a hundred emails. "It was amazing," she says. "Some of the stories were really well written."

Maryn is hiding her dog in the bathroom because one of the apartment's workmen is doing some work for her and she isn't supposed to have a dog. The dog barks from the bathroom every so often because it wants to be part of the conversation, and we go into the bathroom to talk to the dog and tell it to quiet down. After the workman leaves, we take a bottle of wine out to Maryn's balcony and talk about a friend of hers who just had an affair with Woody Harrelson. After hearing what Harrelson said to Maryn about how great his wife and house in Spain were, I tell Maryn I'm hungry and we talk about where to get food, but she says she doesn't want food. She shows me the very complicated chemistry charts she made for her pre-med class and I tell her they look like visual poems and then I go get food.

I walk over to Bridge Street Books to meet Rod and Tom. Rod and Tom have been talking over email about the flarf phenomenon in poetry. Rod says flarf is great. Tom says flarf isn't great. It seems like Tom wants to talk with Rod about flarf more than Rod wants to talk about it with Tom. Rod later tells me that when they talk about flarf, Rod gets really annoyed with Tom.

On the bus coming back from Rod's apartment that night, I tell Tom that the social desires of poets can be broken down into three camps. Some poets are individualists, I say, some are groupists, and some are populists. I say all this loudly because I'm drunk. On the bus I define for Tom the differences between individualists, groupists, and populists, and while I'm drunk it all makes sense.

Back at his place, I ask Tom about how things are going with the community of poets in DC. He says he doesn't know because he's been staying away from everyone. The next day while he's at work, I get a long e-mail from him telling me why he's been staying away. He prefaces the e-mail by saying it's easier for him to talk about things sometimes if he can do it over e-mail.

Rob and I (Rob shouldn't be confused with Rod) go to lunch at Ollie's Trollie. Rob says that at the IRS where he recently started working, no one understands why he lives in DC. Some people don't even understand *that* he does. He tells them where he lives and they say, "You mean Fairfax?" He says no, DC. They say, "When are you moving?"

I say to Rob that living in North County San Diego, I'm always trying to decide which parts of the local mentality are just generally suburban and which parts are specific to San Diego County. "There's a belief in absolute subjectivity with a spiritual dimension linked to a corporate Republican culture, and that may be unique," I say. "On the other hand, I could just be getting this from the *Los Angeles Times*."

Every few minutes the next morning, WTOP News talks about the fallout from the shutdown of east coast corridor train service on Amtrak. Thousands of people are stranded in Washington, Philadelphia, and New York, WTOP says. WTOP says Amtrak is saying that the shutdown has been caused by an electrical short, but according to WTOP, Amtrak says it doesn't know what caused the short. I listen closely because I have to go to New York on Amtrak in a couple days.

In various private and public Internet conversations, some of which I'm part of and some of which I get told about, some poets are accusing other poets of being frat boys. In the world of poetry, that's a big putdown. Even some women poets are getting called frat boys. I had used the term "frat boy Dada" when I had been at the Miami of Ohio conference, and over the next few days I notice that other people I know are saying it.

On Rod's balcony, I talk about war movies with Kaplan, Doug, and Rod. Kaplan and Doug like Kubrick's *Paths To Glory,* but Rod says he's skeptical that the movie could be better than *All Quiet On The Western Front.* Kaplan says some of the scenes in Kubrick's film really shocked him. "I kept hoping the movie would take me to a better place," he says. "It didn't."

I ask Kaplan what he's been reading and he says he's been looking into the field of masculinity studies. I tell him I'm skeptical of masculinity studies. I'm not sure they're studies, I say, I think they're just putdowns. Kaplan says there's one book by a woman that identifies multiple types of masculinity. I ask, what are her conclusions? Kaplan says she concludes that the field needs further study.

Melanie tells everyone on Rod's balcony that she's going to the store for pods. "I knew it," I say. "I moved to San Diego and now all my DC friends have been taken over by aliens and worship pods." Mel explains that pods are something she uses to make coffee, but I don't drink coffee and say I won't accept the explanation. I point at something she's holding in her hand. "Is that a pod?" I say. "Are you worshiping it right now?"

The next day, my father and I talk about packing some boxes of books I've left in his office and will be moving by UPS to California. There are several different size boxes and we talk about which size is the best to send books. Ultimately we use boxes of different sizes. What the UPS website says confuses me, but when I call UPS information, the guy on the phone just quotes words from the website back at me. I say, "But those words don't make sense. Can you explain what that means?" The guy on the phone again quotes the words back at me.

Walking to his apartment, where I'll be staying a few nights, Dan and I talk about academic job interviews and how they're organized. Dan explains that at his university, where I used to work, the credentials of every candidate had to be passed around among a committee of three. A candidate needed two people to vote yes in order to make it to the next round. Ultimately the finalists were ranked in order of the committee's preference and then were invited to campus for a day-long interview. Dan says the person whom most of the committee wanted bombed in the classroom, and a person not many of them wanted did much better, and the committee had a long discussion about it. Dan says he ended up with a tie-breaking vote and decided to pick the person who could teach over the person who could write. "I didn't want to become known as the one who hired a lousy teacher," he says.

Dan and Rod and I are driving to the Washington Nationals game and we talk about getting hot dogs and sausages and beer. We talk about Mike and why he wasn't able to come with us and Dan does an imitation of Mike's voice saying, "Sausages? Whaddya you guys talking about, sausages?" At the stadium some boys are trying to walk around the whole upper deck. Two stadium guards stop them right below where I'm sitting, talk to them a minute and point them back in the direction they came. I lean forward in my seat, trying to hear what the guards are saying, but the stadium noise is too loud. Dan and Rod and I keep trying to guess what the final score of the game will be.

A huge man ordering in front of me in one of the stadium's concession lines shouts, "Two large hot dogs. And give me a big mouth beer."

After the game we meet up at the bar The Black Cat with a number of Dan's friends as well as a few friends of mine. Rod and Mel and I ask Chris questions about Jean Genet, and Chris says that Genet is an essential canonical figure in gay literature and that may be why Chris never talks about him anymore. I ask Olga, a former student of Dan's, whether she's staying in town for the summer and she says yes. She says she doesn't like to go home and see her parents. She says that when she told her parents she wanted to major in English, they told her she'd have to pay for it herself and now she's working to do that. It's kind of a relief, she says. We talk about writing and I say that it's important to approach writers like regular people and not try all the time either to suck up to them or put them down. "Some writers are obnoxious and others aren't," I say. "You have to take them on a case to case basis like anybody else." Sara is talking about entering a program in publishing in Denver, where she'll be for six weeks. After the program she's going to New York City to try to get a job in publishing. "But I think maybe I want to be a professor," she says. "I like the kind of life they live." Dan and I get loudly skeptical about the lives of professors, because we are professors and have that sort of life and on the whole it's not so great. Others at the table say that our lives don't seem so bad, especially since our jobs allow us at least a little time to write, and I'm forced to admit that my life isn't actually all that terrible. I don't like admitting that my life isn't bad, I tell everyone. "It may seem all right on the outside," I say, "but when you're on the inside, my brain is there, and I don't think any of you want to live with my brain."

Dan and I go to breakfast the next morning and talk more about jobs and about the party that night at Dan's. We go into detail about the party arrangements, drinks and food, who will be there and what those people are like. Dan's girlfriend Stephanie is arriving from New York on a bus for the party, and he says he'll call me when he's picked her up and I can meet them at his apartment, where I've been staying. He calls me several times that afternoon to say her bus hasn't yet arrived, but eventually he calls to say it has and I can meet them at the apartment.

At the party that night, a lot of people talk about a lot of things but most of it I don't remember the next day when I try to write it down. I remember talking with Magnus about the Yockadot Poets Theater Festival, with Adam about how he and his girlfriend Kat, who's currently in Uganda, have decided to get married. Ryan and I share the jokes we know about California. I ask people if Kaplan looks more like a student or a professor. I talk to Suzannah about Mike and what he wants for the future, and Suzannah says Mike doesn't know what he wants. Mike and Rod and I share a tequila shot and talk about tequila, how it's a healthful drink that connects people to the earth, at least that's my theory anyway. I talk with Cathy about something I can't remember, with Tom about something I can't remember, and with Olga about something I can't remember, although I remember telling her that she was brave to strike out on her own, and I make some joke about "the essential Russian soul" which is something that Dostoevsky used to talk about, and Olga tells me I'm stereotyping Russians and I say I don't think I am. The next morning when I go to brunch, a little hungover, with Dan and his girlfriend, I talk about how it's hard to remember the things one talks about at parties. I ask Stephanie whether there was a bad song she heard at a lot of parties in the last year, and if so, what song was it, but she says she didn't go to parties all that much.

Sitting on Rod's balcony that evening, Doug tells a story about being bitten by a translucent scorpion. He was in Greece and had passed out from drinking too much, and in the morning he had been bitten by something but didn't know what. Then he saw the scorpion, almost clear in color, scuttle across the floor. Doug emphasizes the word "clear" and "scuttle" so that we understand what it's like to have a hangover and see a translucent scorpion run across the floor when you realize it's bitten you. Doug then tells a story about taking a crap in the outhouse one afternoon. That night at dinner, one of the Greeks said to him, "You didn't actually shit in our well, did you?" Doug, embarrassed, and afraid that he had mistaken the well for an outhouse, denied it. All the Greeks laughed at him, Doug says, because several of them saw him go to the outhouse, which really was an outhouse and not a well. Doug says, "The Greeks sure did have a lot of fun with me."

At my parents' house, my mother hands me a letter from her sister, my aunt officially although I've never thought of her that way, which talks about the things she and her family have been doing. My mother's sister's daughter has epilepsy, and the letter says her daughter is currently getting good care for the epilepsy. My mother's sister says in the letter that she still enjoys riding her motorcycle and that her husband enjoys watching The History Channel.

My father and I talk about how to set up his new computer at home and how to get it online and virus protected. A computer check of his old computer says his virus protection hasn't been updated for more than two years. I explain to my father that this makes his computer unprotected from viruses.

Since I've been moving around a lot, I haven't had much chance to hear the news and I don't miss it. Tom tells me that media predictions are calling for a close race between Busby and Bilbray for the southern California congressional seat vacated by Randy "Duke" Cunningham, who's now in jail for fraud. I tell Tom I don't believe what the media is saying, that no matter how corrupt Cunningham was, in North County San Diego the election of a Republican is inevitable. Never mind, I say, that Bilbray too has been connected with financial scandals. In North County San Diego, I tell Tom, the newspapers say that

Democrats are always corrupt, and that when Republicans are corrupt, that's because they've become infected by Democrats. Do you understand, I say to Tom, that all this means that in San Diego County, a criminal Republican is by definition a Democrat?

After each poet finishes reading at the poetry series at Bar Rouge, Carly and Reb, the two women who host the series, start yelling, "Take it off." The poet is supposed to take off a piece of clothing and auction it to the audience, and the money becomes the poet's pay for the evening. Jamie, who read several poems with his friend Jon that were discussions with online robots, auctions off a sock stuffed in his crotch. Daniel, who read several poems about his crotch, auctions off a sweaty Hawaiian shirt. People actually do shout out bids and pay for the clothing items in question. Some of the audience who don't bid talk about the ridiculousness of the bidding; is it a fun gimmick or another silly attempt to make poets seem fashionable or like rock stars? One pretty dark-haired woman in an fancy black evening dress, sitting at the bar talking with Carly, who's also the bartender and clearly her friend, bids relentlessly on both auctioned items and wins one. When I go up to get a drink, Carly talks to me about some of the drinks she's been pouring. I tell the dark-haired woman, "You're a plant," and she says, "No, a lily." Then Jamie and Adam and I talk about poetry, politics, and theory. I claim that some poets, like Jeff Derksen, have a definite and developed theory about politics, and others, like Kevin Davies, do not. Adam says that not having a definite theory about politics is still a theory. I say no, I don't think it is. But we don't reach any conclusions about whether it's better for a poet to have a theory about politics.

I'm sitting on the Amtrak the next morning, waiting to leave DC for New York City, and a woman several rows behind me tries to put a large suitcase on the rack above her head. She says to a woman standing next to her, "Some people are helpful and others just aren't." I look around, trying to see if she's making that comment about someone in particular, maybe even me, but if she is, I can't tell.

Once in New York, I talk to Ethan on my cell phone and he says he wasn't expecting me until the following night even though I had emailed him otherwise. We talk on our cell phones about how hard it can be to talk over email and while we're talking, the music playing in the CD store where I'm standing keeps getting louder and it's hard for me to hear what Ethan is saying. I go out on the street, hoping it will be quieter, but there's construction on the street and it's even louder, so I ask Ethan if he can call me back in a few minutes when I've walked to a place where I can hear him. I walk to a corner of Union Square where it's at least a little quieter and wait for Ethan to call back. When he does I say, "It's very hard to talk on the phone in New York, isn't it?"

After we talk on the cell several times about where and when to meet, I meet Ethan at his reading at the Bowery Poetry Club. At the club I talk to Ethan and his girlfriend Kim, to Rob and to Kenny, and to a poet I don't know who's in town from Seattle for a reading and a play that he's in. I talk for a moment to Kristin, who's holding her baby, and in front of the club briefly also to Alan, who's the father of the baby, although I'd recently been told that Kristin and Alan have split up. I go to dinner with Ethan and there we meet Carol, Sue, Natasha and Alison, and I talk to all of them. In New York, sometimes it seems I'm so busy talking to everyone that all I can remember is who I talked to and not what I said. Carol has a new book that talks very well about the connections between contemporary politics and her personal life, and Carol and I talk about working too much and never getting to talk to people and why we feel like we have even less time to talk to people than we used to. Another thing I notice about New York is how when I'm there, I'm often talking to people about who they're talking to and everybody always says they don't have time to talk to anyone. But I tell everyone at dinner what it's like in San Diego and everybody is kind to me and oohs and aahs at the outrageousness of my stories. They tell me they find my stories about San Diego shocking. Lots of people I know in New York always say they're shocked about what goes on in the rest of the United States, but I feel like they find being shocked pleasurable because it reminds them they're in New York. So I'm always trying to shock them because I want them to be pleased and entertained. I tell them all how happy I am to see them.

Shane Roeschlein

Genesis

Dawn. Low earth orbit.

The satellite's photo voltaic cells mirror the curvature of the earth's atmosphere inducing a chiaroscuro of its fuselage and telemetry antennae array. As it moves incrementally from darkness to light a bay door opens and an innocuous mechanical assemblage emerges from its darkened recess.

The onboard camera resolves in a resolution of 25cm. Producing an image of stunning clarity from approximately six hundred kilometers in the sky. When commanded it can focus grid-like on any given location: a city street; the sequence of numbers on a license plate; wing coverts of a pigeon perched on a wire.

It has established a complete photographic documentation of the earth.

Ignition...

The eleven rings of the Bessel beam push the cells into a protean chorale. Cellular harmonics lift the spectrum into new verticalities of energy.

They also push.

They pulse and plush.

It is immaculate, rigid, and unbroken. A perfect, self-healing cylinder.

The azure ray extends downward. Earthbound.

On the planet's surface there is silence as the simulation renders. The illusion extends laterally and medially across continents and oceans.

God's bated breath.

Kenneth Bernard

#39 from Malone Dies Poems

39. "In the case of mules it is the eye that counts, the rest is unimportant. So he looked the mule full in the eye at the gates of the slaughterhouse, and saw it could still be made to serve."

S. Beckett, *Malone Dies*

but why only mules
cannot humans do too
a quick stab in the eye
and recognition's truth
you'll do old girl
no knacker'll get you
while I need
not too many tussles
but a lot of work
be you bony or a fat arse
your eye won't lie
and we'll do it
cozy as two bugs
eking out the years

too grim you think
I'll tell you grim
jabbering to beat any band
that tells the tune
I don't dance and I don't sing
but I know need
and so I think do you

the rest don't matter
if your eye is true
I know potato minuet
and laugh a sneer
and now I've caught you in a smile
no slaughterhouse for you
no matter what they've said
who's they you're asking
the whole world's they
and they don't know dry turd
but we know something
and eye to eye we'll walk away
leaving maybe a fart or two
to help them procreate

just don't yet die
and I promise I won't lie
I've seen your eye
we're done with knackers
and their place of work
this world this realm
that stink to high heaven

Andy O'Clancy

Facebooked

At present a new discovery, a new machine, is at work to turn the attention of men back to a visual culture and give them new faces; [...] The silent film is free of the isolating walls of language differences. If we look at and understand each other's faces and gestures, we not only understand, we also learn to feel each other's emotions.

—Béla Balázs

She is the shape of my lens.

—R.Gus

future terrorists

No one reported that the armored cars had been sent for. The clocks never struck thirteen, there were no decaying houses painted in infinite gradations of gray, pearl and off-white, no smoke and bullets or commander shooting himself in front of the troops, bits of debris were not littered far and wide, no fertilizing rooms ever universally hatched uniform batches of standard women and men, and not all the buildings were made of glass, proclaiming to be permeable. Still, civilization had long ago abandoned itself.

And what will become of habitual whispers of this hour now remembered, while records, documents, and other memoirs fade like day-old footprints on dry desert sand, she thought.

People moved unlike ants or bees, with no mother; scrabbling upon decentralized plateaus, smiles and grimaces—the face—their only legitimization.

[This section/chapter will be from the perspective of Justice at JFK airport moments before being apprehended (you read her trial with the last submission). Even as you read, efforts continue in breakout groups of independent federal agencies like the National Science Foundation and other Western countries attempting to use emerging technologies to locate, organize, and interpret faces for "commercial" potential. Just to mention a few examples: Computer scientists at one of the recent "New Ivies," the world-renowned Robotics Institute at Carnegie Mellon University, and the "Affect Analysis Group" at the Research lab at the University of Pittsburgh have formed an interdisciplinary research team for facial expression analysis by computer processing. They were crucial in helping to place those cameras at INS passport control booths at major airports spotting *known* terrorists on international watch-lists. However, they also have plans of prophecy. That is, monitoring and interpreting facial signals regarding deception or attitude (i.e., detecting future terrorists using algorithms to extract facial-expression and body-gesture as *indicators of intention* and deception for a remote sensor system using video sources), boredom or inattention in workplace situations. Such metaphors convey the camera's supposed abilities as a mechanism of knowledge, as a new ocular instrument stripping the veil from the face of objects to a previously imperceptible reality. Facial configuration relations between subjects are spatially dependent, and therefore represent temporarily determined phenomena produced according to someone or something else as a model. Consider Fanon's response before this sort of technology became available: "I am overdetermined from without. I am the slave not of the 'idea' that others have of me, but of my own appearance. [...] And already I am being dissected under white eyes, the only real eyes. I am *fixed*. Having adjusted their *microtomes*, they objectively cut away slices of my reality" (*Black Skin White Masks*, 116). Originally, *microtomes were* late nineteenth-century instruments for microdissection. We are now back to the surface, to the tissue always ready to be dissected, collected, categorized, classified. While subsequent microtoming techniques have altered significantly, the intellectual apparatus embedding distorted forms still bear the same distinct knife marks. Because facial casts within these convergences can never be independent of some sort of spatial scale, approximating complexities to make character pronouncements indicates a perpetual driving problem this section of *Groundless Revolution* will explore]

fake viewfinder

Safely concealed within his electrically charged enclosure, surrounded by the blinding whiteness of the same eight-foot high walls where he'd been tirelessly guarding the sacred cow of his culture by manning the control booth for facial expression analysis through computer processing at JFK for nearly five years, he knew the proper procedure. He trained one of the greenhorns only this afternoon before clocking in, repeating FEA instructions from memory almost verbatim:

"First you take a facial enhancing lens and fold over the fasteners as indicated on the container. Then you take part 3 and, using mild pressure, fix it to your completed section 1 at point X, where you see the tiny hole. Attach the small sections of part 2 to section 1 before sticking the sections together. From sections 1 and 2 take the outer parts and stick them together from inside with section 3; then stick this section to the front of 1. Now after sticking the whole "lens" to the viewfinder, you simply mark the acceptable passengers and other fellow travelers by pressing this button. BE CAREFUL! We are compelled to inspect vigilantly every face, every physiognomy that attempts to pass our way. This is an intuitive operation that depends on accuracy! And you know the satisfaction we take in that facility which gives more meaning, more consequence to life for us than for those monitored."

Good Seeing, he called it. Supplementing technological observational quality. Afterwards, he figured that he had initiated the neophyte well enough, and he went to his assigned control booth. Nearly five hours passed before he realized he had not eaten.

Horrors! Lunch at 8 pm. In this spotless hole of perpetual monotony.

"So you would like to know why I hate you today?" he alleged aloud, gazing at the compliant funeral procession making its way through the updated airport. As far as he was concerned, its architectures effectively designed the structure to induce confidence despite the incomprehensible resentment of zealous imbeciles, and his furtive duty within its intentionally soothing atmosphere amplified this. Connecting these social engineers to his own station, he considered the thankless piety of countless anonymous craftsmen who, with venomous satire, sculpted the Disney-like prison for the legions of grotesque, monstrous figures scattered across nearly every walkway, seat and ledge. Still, his thankless task was unenviable and absurd, and he knew it.

Avoid Mondays and bad weather.

Then, like a creeping presence lying behind the curtain in a puppet show full of holes, he bit into his pickle sandwich and, via the many cameras conspicuously placed throughout the airport, traced his lens across the thickly clotted gulf of space through vague clatter, drinking, dancing, snake handlers, juggling balls, and Jesus Jumpers jumping for Jesus, until, almost immediately, he caught sight of a familiar face midway between change on a rotating advert for the latest reality show. Lounging on a bar stool with three other men near the billboard, their faces reflecting desperation, infection, and plague, the human version of this hollow figure motioned via acrobatic eyebrow movements and variations of mouth holes for the others to observe the splendidly attired mystical letters of the ad floating toward their eyeballs with the occult effect of stars while drinking from a bottle of Midleton Irish Whiskey:

"It all started as a goddamn experiment, you know. I was just going to do this shit for 202 days. But what you might take into account is that when I was on those shows talking about being off whiskey and drugs, I was still on them. It's a level I'm very proud of.

"Indeed!" one replied.

"Come!" rejoined another. "Transmit windspeak with us—use your cognitive mush to push tree breath through your vocal chords while fashioning no less than gymnastic wonder with your throat and tongue to produce audible waves of patterned sound into the atmosphere, which I may discern as some sort of halfway entertaining thought or idea for love's sake—say something, damnit, say something, man! Say something that professes to mean something; all that work and wheel—make it good!"

"And, just for the record, bizarre is as billed," the third countered. "I propose a toast," the entertainer bellowed. "Let's pay homage to the long vanished sun of Art."

"And all that other shit sure to land each of us in the grand furnace."

"Salud then—to being born with monkey asses!"

No longer wanting to concentrate on this rotting atrocity, he trained his lens toward the cross-section of travelers waiting in the vicinity of the next arriving flight. Near the trashcan by the bathrooms he saw the war-crippled remains of a veteran sitting alone in a crumbling wheelchair. He was missing one leg and part of an arm. He also noticed that the medals the man proudly wore on his chest matched the color of the small coins people dropped in his begging cup, which he extended with a trembling hand. It was easy enough to see the fake nose and the scars across his cheeks and lips, but these traumatic dislocations did nothing to evince the veteran's discontent, which went unnoticed until running a Facial analysis that also revealed the man's tear-filled left eye was false.

Still and all, he thought after checking the computer analysis, *despair, deception, and disillusionment do not equal direct action.*

He told himself personal bias had nothing to do with running the mischievous faces of two children laughing together like brats near the new fountain; they had sadistically glossy gun mouths, and their four eyes stared too fixedly. He was about to run the worthy woman of about thirty-five, with weary face and slightly graying hair, who stood near the boys carrying a puking little girl on her arm, when a number of deadly serious, hyperbolically muscular men strutted through his lens in tight fitting attire. Disfigured and deformed by steroids, he noticed that they had an almost brutal physiognomy; he decided there was nothing overtly suspicious about them.

"Point is that when they say *shit* they're used to hearing *what color?*"

"It's like my neighbor, supposedly retired Navy; this guy is ousted from his house on a gurney, eyes closed in a neck brace, and you think, 'Oh, hope he's okay, no real family, mostly private, better check up on him, see if he needs anything,' but the only document with a name on it is too far away to make out through the blinded window, so you get binoculars and such, and after more than a little trouble find that the names don't add up, know what I mean?"

"I knew him like a regular simile, like, you know, like, two $.99 tacos and five or more stuffed jalapeños with ranch dressing on a double bacon sourdough cheeseburger with an extra–large French fry, extra-large Coca Cola, and, of course, a $.99 chicken sandwich at 3 am on Saturday night.

Undeviating night blindness, and yet, every word enamored of assurances resembling blessed counsel.

Just then, a coterie of half-costumed-full-drunk Joeys breaking wind and more than a few of the clown code of ethics rules exited the international flight like they were still involved in the tail-end of an all-night game of poker.

"First traveling circus I have ever been in where circus clowns sport clown names outside the ring, Sir Galahad. Not like we are going to be staying in a place long enough to get known by a clown name."

"I used to ride the rails with a dog like you," a hobo clown offered through downtrodden makeup. "One night he fell off the back of a box car."

A thrust. Jabs. Whacks. Socks. Pain—aches and agonies, free record—maybe even a little unplanned coin exchange, until the boss clown, an overly orderly outfitted white face usually responsible for coordinating routines and representing the clowns in business matters, stepped in.

"Now you listen to me!" he shouted, "listen to me good: most clowns don't even know my real name, you understand? Do I care? Fuck you I care! I'm glad my name became sticky, because that's what it takes to make yourself known! Names are important. The point is you don't just start calling yourself Gumdrop because you like gum; I mean do you know how many clowns out there are named Buttons because their costume had buttons? Why do you want to get mixed up with them? Don't be satisfied, desire more for yourself, and go out there with your own representation. That's it. Now go bump a nose next time."

Another clown had apparently separated from the group and was busy defending himself to a college student that had been forced to sit near him on the plane.

"Couldn't you have at least been a Charlie Chaplin, or something like that?" she insisted. "I mean, do you really need to keep glorifying a modern version of an Auguste clown while Ronnie McDonald sells poison sugar–water to children?"

"C'mon, baby, you know you like my wild pink hair, the large red nose, enormous shoes, along with all the other comically exaggerated features I bring to the table."

No need to even run an analysis—with one push of a button the men were apprehended for wearing disguises. He pirouetted the lens to survey the light gleaming through a couple of women in skirts, their faces unmistakably genital.

I want to tuck my luminous body into you all, you know—similar to an asteroid or a comet streaking naked and unhindered through an unsuspecting planetoid, or a solitary splotch inside the boundaries of a bleached black hole.

In the tower where no one was watching, the lens of his ocular instrument stripped the veil from the face of each and every unprincipled, lonely little human exiting the plane, while he listened in on any conversation he wanted. Half-extinguished shadows stretched out from the doorway nearly all the way past the circular information booth, where most trotted briskly along like imprisoned donkeys following a long-established rutted path. Some were confined in elegant clothes or stagnated by murky grins. There were violent yawns, wicked whispers, pleading faces filled with fright, unprincipled profiteers, bestial priests, bedizened senior citizens, and sociable wives with soily jaws.

In the midst of this garrulous clamor, he could hear her lightening as she stumbled out from the airplane departure hall, although she said nothing.

Broad wings make doorways cumbersome.

The surface of her face seemed as lusciously obscure as sunshine on a rainy day, and in her eyes the song of angels radiated. He imagined her parading down a catwalk nebulously tinted white and green when she twisted her way back toward the windows where the wounded night fog obscured the airplane, though he noticed that the light gnawing through the broken pall came from the rotating beacons and auxiliary lights after deforming his vision long enough. He failed to remember his own lunch as he watched her blithely chomp and swallow two crumbly cookies from the plane. The richness of her bliss saturated the entire area. He studied the contours of her shoulders, zoomed in as her abdomen shifted across the screen, and kept the moment when she stepped across to the trashcan to throw away the cookie package under surveillance. He adjusted focal lengths to closely inspect her wiping the crumbs from her knees and pulling at her blouse before stopping to embrace the veteran. In that instant he imagined she could show anyone how to maintain unwearying strength, invent fire, or speak to god.

Who is she? Why is she here/ What celestial mystery has landed her here on this desperately decomposing globe?

He imagined her as… [this will be a list of a wide range of disguises/fantasies]

He reread the memo from last week:

TACTICAL FACIAL NAVIGATION (TFN)

1. For reasons endemic to military operations, TACTICAL FACIAL NAVIGATION (TFN), is currently in the process of integrating all airport facilities with a means of checking the accuracy of all Ground check points facial recognition systems.

a. FEA agents must accomplish all necessary checks, providing course and distance information for cited classed expressions, before entering the results of such checks.

b. In control zones, should an error in excess of $\pm 7°$ be indicated, the use of a ground check may be necessary, and, operating on a line of sight principle, may be conducted without first attempting to correct the source of the error.

The use of a ground check may be necessary...

An optimal mouth image was called for, and he captured this the instant she yawned.

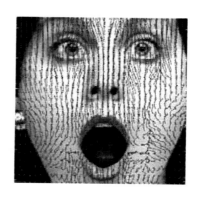

fake buttons [these are not operational]

The badge said Senior Supervisor R.Gus: F.E.A.

"Where are you coming from? What have you undergone, and what places and people have you seen?"

She said she was a dancer and a student. She said she liked sexpositive theory and practice, trash art, and her little pony. She said places traveled presented issues such as economical and social status.

"In no way does globetrotting not require capital," she beamed. "Also spurious, range of scale interpellating designated areas of 'occupied' space and theatrics of homogeneous continuity compulsory to retelling that narrative, e.g., "i've traveled to mexico or france," or, "i've traveled to rhode island or nagaland," as well as multiplicities of heterogeneous lines and other *de facto* prerequisite singular master coordinates, e.g. "i.""

Her naked body was held forth like an uncanny exhibit. Beneath the inked muscled torso of a bloody–looking angel, some **nostalgic Lucida Blackletter** font arched across the apical of her chest like a counterclockwise covenant—a primeval rainbow message tattooed like a low thick necklace illuminating the dimly emerging landscape slowly silhouetted from brilliant darkness over two neatly pierced silver–studded nipples matching the two symmetrically perched through her lower lip: **Death to Cowards Traitors & Empty Words**. The word **Traitors**, the pivot point of that inverted arch, hovering between the first fleshy inclines of modest boobs. The only visible part of the kneeling angel was the zenith of his bald head and the back of his naked, bloody upper torso, his gaze descending in the direction of both hands, themselves palms down, each seized by penetrating barbed spikes above **&**, two majestic wings slouching toward **to** and **Words**. Her left arm slightly sleeved with a little color, a second look revealed witnesses to the tattooed trial upon the shoulder. There was March Hare, holding his Mad Tea Party with the Mad Hatter and the Dormouse. The foundation of their tabletop looked like an endless framed tunnel, the back of two long white ears and a red coat shilly-shallying inward. And there, in a blue and white dress, the side of her face facing the rabbit, her shoulders towards the viewer, was the youthful audacity of Alice—only the cook's hand interspersing between the two, presumably, of course, with too much spice. Two matching golden-eyed blue tigers with serpent-like tails situating toward her underarms and lining the lowermost side of each rib right down to the uppermost part of her hips, open fangs hinting toward empty space above her unshaved badge (lighter than the dyed black hair harmonizing the matching horn-rimmed glasses she wore), which he imagined she was sometimes fond of teasing lovers with by slipping one end of those specs in. He could not see what the tigers' ribbons said.

One had the words 𝕬𝖓𝖎𝖒𝖆𝖑 𝕷𝖎𝖇𝖊𝖗𝖆𝖙𝖎𝖔𝖓, the other, 𝕿𝖍𝖗𝖔𝖚𝖌𝖍 𝕯𝖎𝖗𝖊 something, 𝕿𝖆𝖈𝖙𝖎𝖈𝖘, he thought.

   She said, "Whether a person is a criminal or a public servant must surely be simply a matter of perspective."

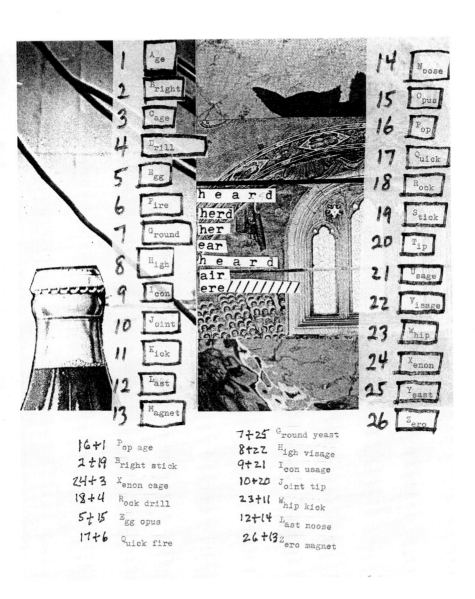

1 A_{ge}
2 B_{right}
3 C_{age}
4 D_{rill}
5 E_{gg}
6 F_{ire}
7 G_{round}
8 H_{igh}
9 I_{con}
10 J_{oint}
11 K_{ick}
12 L_{ast}
13 M_{agnet}

14 N_{oose}
15 O_{pus}
16 P_{op}
17 Q_{uick}
18 R_{ock}
19 S_{tick}
20 T_{ip}
21 U_{sage}
22 V_{isage}
23 W_{hip}
24 X_{enon}
25 Y_{east}
26 Z_{ero}

h e a r d
herd
her
ear
h e a r d
air
ere

16+1 P_{op} age
2+19 B_{right} stick
24+3 X_{enon} cage
18+4 R_{ock} drill
5+15 E_{gg} opus
17+6 Q_{uick} fire

7+25 G_{round} yeast
8+22 H_{igh} visage
9+21 I_{con} usage
10+20 J_{oint} tip
23+11 W_{hip} kick
12+14 L_{ast} noose
26+13 Z_{ero} magnet

TV Demons

Saturday night was so hot, Keiko tossed and turned on the couch, just a shirt across her body and two fans going. She lives alone—who's going to see? Towards morning she fell into a deep sleep and dreamed she was back in Japan, eight years old, walking to school from the farm and getting pinched through the holes in her clothes by other kids. They yelled something over and over, but she couldn't understand what they were saying.

"Mom!"

She opened her eyes but all she saw was the couch back. When she looked up over her shoulder her beloved oldest son was staring at her, terrified.

"What's wrong, Charles?" Then she realized she had only her shirt on and it barely covered her.

"Mom! I came in with my key and saw you lying there!"

Surprised, she almost laughed. Maybe he thought she was dead? "Hand me my kimono, Charlie, last night was so hot! I'm so ashamed—you could have seen my *oshiri*. Please wait in the kitchen and I'll make you some tea."

He throws her the kimono with the green bamboo print, and goes to wait for her. When she joins him, his handsome face still looks red.

"Mom, maybe you should come and live with us—I built you that granny flat, all your own, with a big TV—I worry about you by yourself here."

"Your sister wants me to live with her too, Charles. But I like my house; I don't want to live with my kids like an old lady—I'm fine here."

"Well, at least you could get some air conditioning in this place! I'm going to call the guy who did my house and get it put in. Okay?"

"Oh, Charles, you're so good to me." What would he say if he knew she *liked* to take off her clothes? Liked naked sun baths on her back porch? And his girl-friend Sally might think she's getting the Alzheimers, you never knew. Still, they tried to be nice. And she was so proud of Charles; he'd been a widower for the past four years, raising two girls, and now he's a vice president where he works. She'd asked him what his firm did, but when he started talking about IT this and computers that, she gave up.

As they drank tea she noticed it was eight-thirty—almost time for water aerobics. "I'm late for my exercise, Charles, or I'd make breakfast."

"That's okay, Mom, don't forget you're coming to our house tonight to take care of the girls. I just stopped by to remind you on my way downtown."

"I remember, I'm going to bring some oranges off my tree. And ramen—they love my noodles. And tomorrow we'll celebrate Kim's birthday, I'll make sukiyaki. But Charles, I hate those video games they play so much. I never get a chance to tell my stories any more."

"I'll make sure they put them away tonight. And as soon as I get some extra time I'm going to tape your stories and put them on CDs. Nobody's had a life like yours, Mom."

Keiko smiled; she admired her handsome, successful oldest son. Too bad she couldn't fix him breakfast. Funny, when she was young she could never get enough to eat; now it's easy to wait.

She saw him off, put on her suit and towel and drove to the pool. Later she'd have lunch at the all-you-can-eat Chinese buffet with her girlfriend. *Poor Yasuko, older than me, eighty-six already, she's really got the Alzheimers, I have to tell her not to pay twice. Oh, she watches too much TV—I think it makes her brain mushy. But we have fun at the buffet; I like the chicken and crab, the daikon, and those fried shrimp. Those are not so bad for you….*

Driving, she worried about her dreams: those damn kids when she grew up, pinching her like that on the way to school; she got tired of beating them up. Finally she'd just climb a certain tree and stay in it for hours—that's why she only got two years of school. What was the other dream? Something about being in the pool and the water was too hot, it made her mad. *They say that dreams are trying to tell you something. Maybe I ought to stay home from the pool today?*

But she loved the water. Lots of times Keiko exercised alone in a shallow corner of the pool, watching other ladies talk to each other. After fifty years here Keiko was definitely an American, got her citizenship thirty-five years ago, but sometimes she couldn't understand American women; they acted just like people on TV. Keiko had no interest in movies and shows—she liked sports: baseball, football, sumo wrestling. Charles had been a football star in high school.

Things that really happened to her, Keiko—you never saw that on TV. And in the pool when some women came over to exercise with her, and she started talking about her childhood in Japan, the strange way she got married, her kids and life in Hawaii, Minnesota, and here in California, how amazed they were, sometimes they laughed like crazy, sometimes they were shocked and felt sorry.

Still, today she was in a funny mood. Last time, two women near her in the pool were talking about a vampire movie. Who cared about that stuff? It made her wonder what they saw when they looked at *her*—some old lady who can't afford fancy clothes or even speak as good as they do? *Let them think what they want, they don't have to know about my money or my stocks—people can be really mean if they are jealous.* So in general Keiko talked about her hardships—made them seem funny—and her flowers and travels; it entertained them. *And if they don't want to listen, so what? They can kiss my oshiri.*

At the pool she parked near that young woman Rita, just getting out of her white Toyota, and hurried over. "Oh Rita, how are you today?"

"Okay I guess, but I found out I have high blood pressure and high cholesterol—my doctor put me on a diet of foods that are good for you. Things like fish, greens, shitake mushrooms, blueberries, sweet basil...."

"Me too, Rita, my blood pressure went up too. My doctor says I have to stop eating soy sauce—too much salt! That can be dangerous when you're my age. But I love soy sauce."

"You know, there's a low-salt soy sauce you can buy in the grocery store."

"Is there? Rita, every time I talk to you I learn something new, that's what I like about knowing you."

The young woman looked surprised, as if she wasn't used to compliments, but she smiled back. Keiko, though, meant it.

You have to be smart to stay healthy. How old is Rita? I think about thirty-six, but she looks younger. She encouraged me to sign up on a tour to Paris—the one place I've never been. Rita says their food is interesting—that's what she said: "delicious and interesting!" I could try some of those snails they make. See if they're any different than the ones I used to catch and eat for myself.

Keiko's father died fighting in China months before she was born, leaving his wife and daughters to work alone on their farm. The older girls married young, but Keiko stayed with her mother. She remembers being hungry all the time, catching snails and later snakes in the fields to cook for herself. One day her oldest sister arrived with her husband and locked Keiko and her mother out. "You have to live in the barn now," they said. And Keiko and her mother endured that too.

In the dressing room she saw their instructor changing. "Hello, Carol, nice to see you, how are you today?"

"Fine, Keiko, it's nice to see you too. Hi, Rita."

Keiko didn't need to change, so she went directly out into the morning air, cool near the water. She felt a little hungry and wondered if Rita and Carol really liked her. If only she were easy and confident like them—they were really nice, not phony like the women on TV. So many women she met seemed just like actors. Keiko didn't care for that. When those women smiled, they seemed to be baring their teeth at her.

I've been on my own almost all my life, working, finding food for myself, taking care of my kids—no one but my mom ever worried about me, and I didn't need those other people. So why do I care?

She got in at the shallow end and jogged to the other side. Rita emerged from the dressing room and stepped in the pool, making a funny noise when the water hit her thighs. It made Keiko want to laugh—Rita was such a baby. When Keiko was little, all the kids in her village went swimming in the river, summers, no matter how cold the water, boys and girls were all naked together. She never thought about the difference, but she was tougher than the boys, could almost always beat them in a race.

So much has happened since then. When Keiko was fourteen they wanted her to marry an ugly old farmer and work for him, so she decided to run away to Tokyo: it meant she would have to be dead to the family, to save their honor. Her mother went with her for a mile or two and watched till she disappeared, running to the railroad. How could she ever guess that she would come to America? Today she admitted to herself that America changed her. The tough little tomboy became shy, and even now she sometimes felt like an unwanted stranger.

For Keiko and her kids, America did not become the land of milk and honey—not while she was married. Karl would scarcely give them enough to buy groceries. How could he be so mean?

Now she watched Rita paddle up to the deepest end by herself, not part of the group. Keiko liked the way she kept private, but wished the young woman would stay with her sometimes and listen to her stories.

They say she teaches mathematics in high school. I never even took a class in arithmetic. When I came here I couldn't speak their language and had to learn everything—but I learned it! And when that old man I worked for left me his house, I went to night school and found out how to keep my money. I guess if you can manage your money, you're smart enough.

How strange it was the way she met Karl when the American soldiers came after the war. In Tokyo she was renting a room from a distant cousin and worked as a cook in a restaurant. For five years she took leftover food home to reheat for her dinner on a little stove.

Karl began to come to the restaurant once a week to eat steak, but he never saw her in the kitchen. One Christmas he brought a box of chocolates "for the cook." Keiko had never tasted chocolate before. At home she ate the whole boxful. The next time he came, he asked the owner, "How'd he like the chocolates?" The owner said, "He's a she." That's how they met.

Karl, tall and blonde, born of Swedish immigrant farmers in Minnesota, steady and solid, took a fancy to Keiko. He kept asking her out, but though they often went to the movies, she never let him get close. Her mother once told her, "If a

79

man wants to give you nice things, don't let him—you'll get a watermelon in your belly!" Keiko didn't understand that, but it sounded bad, and she never forgot it.

She was so young and ignorant then! One time Karl gave her a ring, one of those prizes that came out of a Cracker Jack box, and she wore it until her cousin's wife said it was a real diamond and meant she was engaged. That made her angry, and it took a lot of persuading from Karl, her cousin and his wife, before she accepted. After two years in Tokyo they moved to Hawaii; there she realized that this seemingly steady man was in fact a really heavy drinker: he could consume enormous quantities of beer and only act a little slow. She spent the four years on that island having children. There she began to oppose him; her first step was to learn to drive in secret. When he missed meals, she would eat his portion, though she gained weight.

Just after she began to take a class in spoken English, he moved the whole family to his parents' farm in Minnesota. Keiko couldn't understand a word they said. She set about learning the language by watching early morning soap operas on the TV. With his family she acted timid and polite; the mother looked like Karl—tall and stern, though Keiko laughs remembering the woman's face when she saw Keiko chopping onions—whack! whack! whack!—in the kitchen. That was one cold place, Minnesota, but they had warm heaters and thick clothes and always enough to eat: nothing like life in the barn with her mother. Finally Karl was transferred to California where they bought this house she still lived in, just five miles from the ocean. When she asked for the divorce, all she wanted was the house. For the rest, she could work.

With warm pool water lapping at her, Keiko was lost in memories, forgetting to listen to the instructor. Now she looked around. There was that new lady Mary Ann coming out of the dressing room—a tall blonde. At first Keiko thought Mary Ann was glamorous, like one of those women on TV who play lawyers and doctors and everybody admires. But more and more to Keiko that woman began to seem like a devil who wanted to torment only her. Mary Ann would move from one group of ladies to another, joking and chatting, but she ignored Keiko as if she were invisible. If Keiko was telling someone her stories, Mary Ann would turn her back and move as far away as possible. Why?

What do I care? Keiko thought today, *I don't even like you!*

Usually when aerobics class ended Keiko washed off alone in a private handicapped shower, out of modesty, but today that stall was taken. So there she was in a common shower with Rita, Carol the instructor, a German woman named Greta, and Mary Ann.

That German woman had a beautiful body, slender and full at the same time. It always made Keiko conscious of her own slight frame that carried too much fat, and today Mary Ann seemed to be staring right at her in an unpleasant way.

"Greta, I wish I had your body," Mary Ann exclaimed—"don't you, Keiko?— you must get tired of being so dumpy looking. Where can I buy a body like yours, Greta? The Body Shop?"

Keiko knew that the Body Shop was some kind of dark bar where men went to see women "topless." A kind of electric wave went through her, of shame and embarrassment.

When she saw Greta turn red with anger, it was like a switch turned on in Keiko. "Who do you think you are?" she yelled at Mary Ann. "Who needs to listen to you—you should be ashamed of yourself, talking to people about their figures that way!" With dignified self control, Keiko exited the shower, wrapped her towel around her like a sari, and went out to her car.

Driving home, she had to control herself not to speed. That was so humiliating! Still, why should Keiko feel intimidated? She stood up to that woman. All the difficulties she had overcome, divorcing her drunken husband, working three jobs, bringing up her kids: mostly she felt strong and proud—yet all it took was Mary Ann, the woman who looked like somebody on television, to leave her feeling bad.

Now she remembers that long after the divorce, when she had that job climbing trees to cut branches, Karl called to tell her he was dying; pancreatic cancer he called it. She got time off from work to go care for him in his trailer in Arizona. Before he died they made friends. It made her wonder if she'd been wrong to leave him.

He left five boxes of things he wanted the kids to have. Among them was an oil painting of the barn she and her mother had lived in. It shocked her. He must have gone out there and taken pictures of that place, and years later paid someone to paint it. Probably he'd meant to give it to her—but she divorced him. Karl took her away from poverty and gave her a new life, with her four great kids.

She sighed.

But as she pulled into the driveway she noticed that the first one of her Angels Trumpets had begun to flower, layers of great pink horns as big as her feet, and her spirits bounded back. Today she'd work in the garden, talk to her dead mom's picture at her shrine, meet Yasuko for lunch, go later to Charles' house and babysit the girls. Tomorrow morning she'd take them to the water park— they loved that, make ramen for lunch. For Kim's birthday she'd give fifty dollars to each girl to spend however she wanted, then a special video game for Kim. Sure she hated those games, but that's what Kim wanted. At night everyone in the family would come, and she'd make sukiyaki. Maybe she wouldn't go back to that damn pool for a long time.

Anyway, she had stood up for herself and Greta today.

When old Mr. Hirsch, that rich man who'd hired her to clean house for his wife, found out she could take care of plants, they asked her to try to save their fruit trees—a whole row of them in big pots on the front porch. She talked to those plants and fed them liquid fertilizer; it took months but she brought them all back to life, better than ever. Mr. and Mrs. Hirsch liked to hear her stories about her life and her hardships, and they were good friends all the five years she worked for them.

"Keiko, it's a good thing you weren't born a man," Mr. Hirsch told her once. She looked at him cautiously: "Why?"

"If you'd been a man, we might not have won the war."

That made me so proud, though he was just flattering me, no one could have stood up against their bombs, and besides I was a little girl when all that happened, hunting food to eat, far away from those cities where the bombs fell—thanks for my good luck.

Yes, he made me proud, and if I admitted the truth, I am a very proud person. There's no reason I should be ashamed to go back to the pool and face those ladies on Saturday. I want to bring some avocados to Rita.

Next week she waited near the pool stairs and before Rita paddled out to the deep end, Keiko said in a quiet voice, "Rita, I was so embarrassed when that woman talked about me being fat. I would never talk like that to another person. She had such bad manners!"

Rita looked surprised and relieved at the same time. "I felt the same way, Keiko. By the way, do you really have four kids? It's hard enough having one."

As they started talking, Keiko felt self conscious about her accent, but Rita seemed to understand fine. Keiko's spirits rose.

"Rita, I have some oranges in my car for you, and next week I'm going to bring you a cutting from my angel's trumpet. Mine is in bloom right now—it has more than a hundred blossoms—bright pink."

"What did you say, an English trumpet? Thanks, I'll bring you a chard plant."

Keiko gasped. "Oh! Thank you so much! I remember the chard my mother used to grow outside our house sixty years ago. She'd put it in our miso soup. That will make me so happy!"

"Rita, did you know when I was fifteen I ran away from home so I didn't have to marry an old farmer and work for him like a slave?" she began, and seeing the look of amazement and interest on the younger woman's face, Keiko began telling her about her life adventures.

* * * * * * * * * *

Keiko's Sukiyaki as told to Rita

Put in a pan 1 teaspoon salt, 2 teaspoons sugar, 1 teaspoon of beef fat. Fry until brown. Add ¼ cup sake. Boil really fast with ½ cup soy sauce and ½ cup water. This is your sauce.

Have ready two pounds of beef top loin sliced thin, two bunches of green onions chopped to 1-inch pieces, 8 ounces of sliced mushrooms, and 1 pound of tofu in cubes.

Also boil potato noodles or bean threads for 2 minutes, or until soft, and cut after cooking.

After the sauce is ready and still cooking, dip each piece of beef in it for 30 seconds, then put the beef in separate dishes with the tofu, noodles, mushrooms and onions. You can also add a raw egg to the sauce, then spoon the sauce into each dish over the beef and noodle mixture. Then it is ready to eat.

M. Benedict

M.M.
or
(Day in the Life)

Early Morning -

Rise and shine to tickle of morning wood (mine, not Jim's) throbbing against my thigh. He still tucks his own sex between his legs when we make it. I take him from behind and he says it's just sensational.

Careful not to wake him, I masturbate myself and fall back to sleep in the warm puddle of cum.

Midday -

Give Zanuck his pre-lunch cigar. He takes me in his mouth and chews at the tip. They're only little love nibbles. Jim refuses me oral. After lunch, Zanuck will smoke me again. For the one and only time he swallows, and I shake into one of my visions:

I am making it with lady madonna on set of a western. I am an indian chief and she a cowboy. Though a virgin, she does not bleed. Jesus is behind the camera. I don't need any direction.

Zanuck makes to dangle his tongue down my throat and brings me out of it. He asks why my body is in Hollywood and my eyes are always miles away. I tuck myself back into my skirt and give him a wink.

Afternoon -

Cuddle with muggsie in bed. Jim doesn't allow it so we have to when he's out. Muggs licks my ear and tells me he loves me. Then he moves to my hand. Still licking, he reads my fortune:

You will find much success and soon. All the universe asks in trade is that only it receives your love. Avoid sleep. It is then that you are most vulnerable.

Evening -

Jim brings home a cute small thing who calls herself Liz Taylor. He tells me to take her like I take him. He watches. Makes me call her Jim. It takes me over an hour to orgasm. He is upset. More visions:

Taylor is with child. My child. I lead her on a donkey to nazareth. Familiar nativity scene: only one wise man and it isn't even a man but my grandmother. Her gift to the child is her hands. She places them around his neck and squeezes until the little darling quits his wiggles.

Liz has me in her hands and is masturbating me. I push her away. I decide to call her tomorrow to plan the abortion.

Dinner -

Jim and I eat the usual. He is still upset and we don't speak. He clears the table and finally says, "Jesus, Norma. You couldn't have enjoyed yourself a little more, for me?" I call him a mother fucker. He pouts in bed for the rest of the night.

Midnight -

I fight it off for as long as I have strength but finally I doze off on the couch. I dream:

Naked in a room in brentwood I am visited by Mother Mary (or is it nativity Liz Taylor?). The saintly woman kisses me open mouth depositing a mouthful of pills. I understand. I swallow.

I am unburdened of my sex and it is bottled. It lends its powers to the bottle's liquid. Tributary bottles are marketed and sold as fine parisian perfumes.

Muggsie comes and licks my toes. He guards what remains.

Cyril Dabydeen

The Well

Tired and thirsty he leant forward, bending his head to drink from the artesian well where the ground sloped, almost canting under his feet. He would drink now, my father: he'd been on the winding road for hours bringing his cattle home; and the animals lowed and straggled along, pulling one way, then another, and maybe they sensed something in the darkness. A swathe of light filtered in... from somewhere; and his eyes were playing tricks on him, my father said. Then deliberately he turned on the tap. But *someone* was already there... *drinking?*

The hunched form, shoulders stooped; my father had to wait his turn to drink, see. *We waited to hear more... what else he would say. But he didn't want to tell us.* The one already at the well was taking an unusually long time to drink, wasn't he? And the cattle grew more skittish. A dog barked, ululation everywhere. An ass's distant, but loud, bray next; and the cows grew really nervous, my father hummed to himself. A veil of mist descending... yet darkness was all in intermittent light. My father rubbed his eyes, he had to drink. *Tell me more, Father.*

Lightly he tapped the one before him drinking so long.

A bull pranced impatiently. A tremor in my father; and maybe he wasn't thirsty anymore. The one before him, his shoulders stooped: Who was he really?

My own throat felt parched, like I was the one at the well trying my father's patience, sort of. "You're taking too long," my father rasped. *At me?* The stooped figure turned slowly, deliberately. "The face smiled at me," my father said, he swore. "Manu... no other!"

Really Manu?

"The same I used to know so well." My father's voice a rasp, as he kept telling me, us. But Manu had died six months ago; and almost the entire village had attended his funeral, my father being one of the pall-bearers, didn't I know? And how the women wailed, Manu's wife, Susheila, bawling out her grief. Indeed Manu had been very popular in the village. Clods of earth thrown onto the coffin

I replayed in my mind. Thud-thud. My father's own handful; he really grieved Manu's passing. "Are you sure it was he?" I asked.

My father nodded. But maybe none of us believed him.

The others looked at me, too. The twitch of my father's mouth, his forehead wrinkled. "But you were thirsty and tired," someone said. "Something must have been the matter with you, eh?" Doubtful we all were. Then, "How can Manu be drinking at the well if he... was... *dead?*"

My father shrugged, he couldn't make believers of us.

"It's not true," chimed another.

"Wha' happened next?" I forced the words out, and laughed. The others also laughed, like mimicry.

"What did you do, Gabe?" They called him that, my father.

"Were you still thirsty?" came a soft shriek.

A tremor all around. My father looked at me as he never did before, then at the others one by one. Oh, he would tell me only, wouldn't he? And for days after I would see him looking glum, and, indeed, the cattle were getting to him, more skittish as they seemed each passing day: this work of bringing them home on the long, winding road, sometimes at night. Now something else was on my father's mind; on all our minds, in the village, as the sun's heat began to be almost overpowering; yes, it was the hottest season of the year, it really sweltered.

But Manu, I kept thinking: how well did my father know him? Did Manu really kill himself as had been said? Oh, how Susheila, his wife, had bawled out, the sounds I could yet hear, echoing. The entire village echoing, see.

My father walked around the house, looking forlorn, contemplative in a way I hadn't seen before; as I yet wanted to know everything that happened at the well; the water still running, I heard, and shook my head. Eyes dim, I was becoming anxious, too.

But my father kept silent. He smiled to himself only, and I would look away from him. Odd, I began to harbour a strange fear of him, my own father.

Then he sat with me, with us, and muttered... something, as if to allay the fear. But he couldn't fool me; something was at the back of his mind.

Then before I knew it he was gone again.

Gone?

* * *

The others kept whispering Manu's name, as they told their own stories, this lore more or less. Now about a man on a white horse riding through the village and dragging a chain behind. So eerie! And everyone grew more afraid each passing day and night; they peeped through jalousies and windows to catch a glimpse of the dreaded spirit. *What spirit?* Sugar-plantation time it was, the past coming alive again, with slavery, and white planters chasing after runaway slaves on their horses... at night. Chains rattled louder. When the runaway slaves couldn't stand it any longer, so afraid they were of the dreaded spirits–they gave themselves up. Beaten. Heads lowered, sunken, they returned to do their masters' bidding.

Another tale: an old woman changing her skin, the *ole higue* as she was known in our village, the dreaded vampire?

Not long after my father came home again, and I watched him mumbling to himself. He started sharpening his long-bladed knife, as his lips pulsed: the same knife he carried with him to the backlands. Next he cut the thick head-rope he used to lead the cattle home. He rubbed a calloused finger against the knife's edge to test its sharpness, then sliced through strands of rope. I watched him, thinking. And again the image of the one at the well. *Manu... indeed?*

My father was ready to lead the cattle home, once more. Imaginary, but real. One anxious bull jerked left, then right, I recreated. "Ho, boy," my father called out. "Ho... there," he barked at it. I figured he knew something about to happen, as no one else did. And another lore in me, with us: the *moongazer,* a really tall man who kept looking up at the moon in his steadfast gaze, so close he was to it, his legs spread out, straddling the sides of the street... and whoever passed under him came to his immediate end. *Oh?*

I looked at my father, silent as he was; and he was thinking about Manu, he couldn't fool me; he actually saw him at the well with his shoulders stooped-looking. "Did you really?" I asked nevertheless.

He didn't answer, but hummed. *What?*

"Did you?"

"Did I what?"

"See... him?"

Again he didn't answer. And maybe Manu shouldn't have died the way he did: the way he committed suicide, I figured.

My father's lips moved strangely, throbbing. And Manu didn't like the quarrel he'd been having with his wife Susheila, as was rumoured. The same Manu who'd dress to kill wearing neatly pressed sharkskin trousers, and he combed his hair straight back with the aid of thick Brylcreem. A Bollywood movie-star type he was, everyone said; but movies weren't made where we lived, in Guyana, only in India... far away, so far from South America.

Was Manu disappointed he wasn't living in a place like Mumbai?

Was it what he and Susheila quarrelled about because he wasn't a real movie star? And Susheila would have none of it; she harangued him about going to work in the canefields. And then overnight Manu became gaunt, sad-looking. But some also said he'd been plagued by the *ole higue,* the vampire coming and sucking blood out of him! Not out of Susheila, young woman as she was... as the *ole higue* was famous for doing? Suck the blood out of young Indian women mostly, see. Ah, it was African lore, something since the time of slavery.

Who really believed this anyway? How the others laughed.

I also laughed. And it was how Indians and Africans lived peacefully, together... and were no longer afraid of the *ole higue*, eh?

My father simply hummed, "It was dark, you see."

I looked at him, intensely.

"Maybe I made mistake, Bhoi; it was just my imagination."

I blurted out, "No, father!"

Odd, right then I began thinking about my mother who'd gone away. Ah, the knife in my father's hand... and the cattle lowing, mournfully. The *ole higue*, where was it? "Yes," my father shook his head, "I understand what you're thinkin', son." His moment of affection, maybe; and now he'd tell me more about his own youth, which I yearned to know about... about how from early he'd tended the cattle, always going to the backlands before daybreak; he had no choice because it was the family's way, a tradition sort of.

Once more my father went off to mind the cattle, I conceived, then bringing them home on the long winding trail. And I felt the urge to go with him, I did; but my mother would want me to stay home, thinking I should never be a cow-man.

Again my father took out his long knife and rubbed his calloused finger against the blade; as the knife appeared shiny, lethal. Instinctively I rubbed my eyes. "You see," he said, "that well, I passed by it again today; it had no one near it."

"Oh?" It was daylight, wasn't it?

"No one drink from it anymore, hot as it is."

"Why not?"

He frowned. "Everyone so afraid, Bhoi."

"Who... wha' for?" as if I didn't know.

"That Manu, maybe he still alive," my father winced.

"He cyaan be!"

A dull sound escaped my father's lips. "I was there, see; it was really dark. Just light... from the moon... shining a little," he blinked. "But I was very thirsty, I had to drink." He stopped, he couldn't go on.

"Go on," I yet urged.

Minutes dragged by.

Then he muttered, as if reminiscing: "I was really there when Manu died; I mean, I looked at him... hanging there, as if he wasn't really dead."

Go on!

"He didn't want to die," said my father. "But Susheila, she wanted it to happen." *Wanted what... to happen?* "I saw Manu hanging there, I watched him." Again he blinked; he looked unnatural, my father. Everyone said the same.

Outside in the backyard the cattle lowed mournfully; something they knew with their instinct, those animals. Ah, another long night it'd be with rain threatening, so strange now. Heavy drops began falling on the zinc-topped houses, drumming, and lightning kept flashing, the equator coming closer. Louder the cattle lowed.

Quickly I looked out of the window. My father stood next to me, he did; I felt his breath near me. And the animals were really fidgety, and the flamboyante and cochineal trees swayed their branches; and the knife in my father's hand flickered, the blade luminous, in another flash of lightning. Through the windows of our house, electricity flitted, believe me. And the knife tearing away flecks of flesh, a young bull's, I saw. My father gripped the carcass firmly, then dressed it to perfection. A feast it'd be, a celebration. A wedding?

Whose really? Oh, somewhere, my mother's eyes brightened.

Now I felt I was the one holding the knife and moving it expertly, or just dexterously, tearing away flecks of flesh. And lightning kept flashing everywhere. *I saw a face at the window.* I rubbed my eyes. The knife-blade glinted in the luminous dark. Then the face slowly disappeared. Whose? My father whispered… something.

I merely sighed.

What?

It wasn't anything… real, was it?

I'd sleep soundly that night, as the rain kept pounding, like it would never stop, it would go on forever. Yes, forever.

***

The next morning I went outside the house to see my father at work, the early riser that he was. But now, he wasn't around. The fresh tropical air I inhaled; and the windswept grasses looked greener, and the jamoon tree kept dripping after the rainfall. The roof of the ramshackle barn also dripped, and the ground everywhere was soggy wet with puddles. Slippery… I yet walked along, hopping over ditches.

The sun started coming out, really shining. My father with trousers hitched up to his knees waded through mud and water; he kept goading the animals along as they yet lowed mournfully. "Ho, boy. Ho, girl," he called out. Then, "G'wan!" His voice also an echo in my ears. Then he cursed and pulled out his knife, the blade glinting. Hotter it started becoming, with long days and nights ahead.

…I began going to the well alone, in broad daylight. Then I was thirsty too, I had to drink. I threw one leg after another, moving along in a daze after bringing the cattle home, what I really had to do; and I had to be there too, more thirsty as I kept becoming.

Before the well, I leant forward, hunching my shoulders... and did I expect to be stopped, a hand arresting me? Someone telling me I mustn't drink here!

Manu?

Immediately I wanted my father close by, more than ever.

Clouds overhead, cirrus-formed, and I looked sideways, left and right, and breathed harder. Sounds of beating hooves, cattle in wild commotion, everywhere.

Oh, Gawd! How the animals grew wilder by the minute... because of me?

Trees shook. My father wielding a heavy rope, also; ah, that knife again, glinting. *My throat more parched.* The rope, taut in my hand; as my father stood close by. Crows circled overhead, because of the sun; arabesqued shadows forming on the wavering ground. "Father," I called out.

But he wasn't there. An ass brayed. The villagers' voices I heard, and the mourners in procession. Ah, Manu. Now everyone dared me to call out to my father because he'd been the first to see Manu hanging there when he killed himself, no? *Make no mistake about it.* How the villagers jeered, their mouths opening and closing, then expanding like rubber. And my father had indeed seen the dead alive: seen the *jumbie*, in broad daylight also, didn't he? But he wouldn't tell me. As immediately I thought of my mother... where was she now?

Father, I called out, just as he seemed ready to attack at the spectral form in white before him, attack her with his long-bladed knife, lunge into it.

What form? "It's me," I cried.

But he didn't recognize me, his son. Clouds somersaulted. Crows, vultures, in commotion. Beaks, claws everywhere. Everyone's laughter, too, their shouting becoming a veritable clamour. Blood poured. This final act, my father's. And somewhere was my mother. Susheila too I saw. *Manu, where are you really?*

My father hummed, "You see, that night, Manu had been expecting someone to come to the well." He was sombre, my father. "Maybe Susheila, no one else, a tryst, you see." Ah, Manu being so handsome, movie-star handsome... and so much she loved him, because he was from Mumbai.

My father's eyes burned; he was thinking about my mother only.

He added, "Maybe Manu didn't expect me to be at the well, dead as he was. Oh, he knew, I knew."

Knew what?

My father continued: "Then I pulled the knife... and lunged at him when he turned around... and saw me!" My father closed his eyes. "It happened quickly, I tell you," he moaned. "It really did; but no one would believe me, eh?"

Blood, like an ongoing sacrifice. His words, each syllable, uttered. His own rage no less, everything happening under the equatorial sun, in one life time only, the more I kept thinking about it: in our village, nowhere else.

* * *

A white horse kept dragging a chain behind, all night long; and the *ole higue* vampire with blood pouring from her veins. *Who... really?* "They must believe it's real," my father insisted.

"Believe what?"

"That it was Manu, the one I lunged the knife at, even if it was only into thin air." He stopped, he looked at me. "You never forget a thing like that. *Swoosh...* the knife," he grinned, imitating his swift lunging action once again.

Then my father gripped me by the shoulder, and it hurt; but he wasn't telling me what I wanted to know. *What really?*

Ah, about my mother; and maybe about some place else far from here, if only about India and Bollywood... where Manu really wanted to be.

"Father?" I rasped, rubbing my eyes. Ah, really thirsty I indeed was.

Now I was alone, dreadfully alone, see... at the well, in darkness. Blackness everywhere, even in the sun. Heavy silence all around, as I yet thought about my mother. Slowly I turned, looking back, maybe expecting my father.

Manu!

Tom Whalen

Vampire in Winter

The vampire in winter wonders if he's the Lord of the Universe or only one of His minions. But at base he knows there is only the trinity of the living, the dead, and the living dead. That's all there is. Take it or leave it. Not that most have a choice in the matter. His victims, for example. His victims. Did he lord it over them, or they over him? Desire is addiction only up to a point, and beyond that point, not even I ... No, not even the vampire, the vampire says to himself, need follow the ego beyond pleasure in its uniqueness.

Still what to do with his evening? Stuttgart shivers in its blanket of snow. Surely, down there, someone ... Well, then what? He's not about to beat or be beaten by himself again in chess, at least not so soon after the last time. If it were summer he might be walking down the Uto Quai along Lake Zürich where young women and men lie on the grass staring up at the outdoor screen, a full moon over the lake. Zürich. "Work hard, play hard: everything is casual and first class."

Late one night he found in the Open Air Kino crowd a succulent pair watching ... was it the Hong Kong fantasy *The Heroic Trio?* One chooses, and that night of his vacation he chose this young couple, though the male wasn't, after all, all that young, and after he'd finished him there remained a bitterness at the back of the throat, and the memory of his Russian-accented German. But the young woman—from her patter he gathered she was an American on a Fulbright to study Lenin's months in Zürich—went down like wine.

.

How long without an assistant? But assistants were always more trouble than they were worth. They misplaced the astrolabe, brought in rancid meat. What good? What good? Up and down his penthouse he paces, thinking over and over, What good? What good? His cape ripples out at the bottom with each step he takes on the two-inch thick Turkish carpet. Back and forth he paces.

Somewhere in the building someone is listening to "Moon River" on an iPod. Should he search this certain someone out and drain him? No, no. Best to keep business and home separate. He learned that a long time ago. At least three assistants ago.

He stops pacing, walks on creaky knees to his freezer. The door sighs open like a mesmerized virgin. The vampire reaches into the cold white light of the freezer for a pitcher of blood.

·

The vampire films he sees. The volumes he reads about his species. He wouldn't mind sinking his teeth into some kickass blonde like in the movies. First he would toy with her, spin her like a top on his tongue, then ...

Blah blah blah, how depressing his fantasies are. No killers around to challenge him, at least not of vampires, and the monsters he used to see every few decades—the creature, the mummy, the baby, all his old friends, though he avoided the zombie hordes with their spiked drinks and general bloodlessness— he hasn't seen in years.

·

The vampire's desire for inclusiveness. Some weeks he takes the S-bahn out to Vaihingen and haunts the US Army barracks; other weeks down into the Middle Eastern kettle of Heslach; still others up to the villas near the Kräherwald. One night a CEO in his lounge slippers, a cigar clamped in his mouth, as his eyes widened and the vampire sank his teeth into the lizardy neck. When was that? Late fall, one of his final sucks before winter came on—this blanket of white over the world, his mind.

·

All afternoon he watches from his desk the snow fall.

·

Hours at his language lessons, doing his best to blend in.

·

He could go elsewhere. Tokyo. Kabul. Gdansk. Lagos. Lithuania. A back alley, a bar, a shared drink. No matter. Novelty interests him less these days than metaphysics. Why is that? It must be the winter, it can't be his age. Or could it? Certainly not the state of the world. What state is that? Conditions surround the vampire, but so do they all sentient creatures. Non-sentient ones, too. Yes, he knows about the unreliability of perception.

In his hand he holds a cameo of his mother: her grave white hair, her longevity so deep in her eyes that it's as if nothing is there, a hollowness more hollow than hollow. Into these infinities he plunges and brings back, after his dive, what?

He scratches at a scab on his elbow. Three victims ago (four?), after siphoning a few pints off a child asleep in a stairwell behind a Jugendstil facade on Rotebühlstrasse, he came up for air and cracked his elbow on a banister ornament, a gargoyle whose tongue lolled out of its mouth, as if laughing at the clumsy blood addict. The vampire ripped the creature off its base and sold it the same day to an antique dealer on Schwabstrasse.

.

When a priest in Ulm confessed to the vampire that not even God could stave the soul, the vampire shook his hand and released the priest, not a little worse for the encounter, back into the night. Now he wonders how he could've ever been so sentimental? Who seriously believes, outside the jackal Faith's jaws, the soul exists separate from body? Is thought truly incorporeal or only energy within its corporeal container? *Quatsch*, he thinks, standing at the window, the city a pool of light beneath him.

It's late. These days he sleeps till mid-afternoon.

.

He comes out of the shower shivering, then quickly dries his papery skin, careful not to tear it between his toes and around his thin penis. His fingers, too, are thin, and his lips, his eyes, his mind. Only an elongated figure, he thinks, as he rubs his hand over his tight-cropped hair, his preferred hair style of late.

Around his neck he wraps a plush, warm towel, and sits down with a blood popsicle (vintage: late fall) and the morning paper. A garbage strike in its third week. Good for the rats, creatures he has always had a fondness for. Still, he's thankful that it's the middle of winter, the temperature seldom rises above 0 C. A ploy by the union, perhaps, their generosity in not delaying the strike until summer when the stench would be unbearable.

Elsewhere, the world doesn't look any better; worse, in fact. The news never fails to amuse him. Ah, humanity, he says, then, laughing, swallows the wrong way, and coughs, then can't stop coughing. Like a silly old man, he says, coughing more, coughing his silly head off. This is really ridiculous, he thinks, on his knees now, coughing and coughing. I can't stop.

He really can't. When he tries, the blood he's been breakfasting on surges back into his throat, and he has to swallow again, and again it goes down the wrong way. His head balloons with blood, his throat with bile. He can't stop himself now.

Ahh, please, the vampire moans. Aaagghh, and he coughs again, the bile burning into his septum.

Light explodes in his head, and it's as if he were looking through both ends of a tornado, as if he were experiencing his cosmic finale in some fifties movie or pulp novel.

But he doesn't faint like some silly school girl, not quite. Slowly he rises, pain wracking his old knees (osteo-arthrosis?), then sits down again at the table.

.

Under the microscope, the platelets look a little pale. Too much CO_2 or lactic acid? Something wrong in what he slurped, but he couldn't tell what exactly. To bone up on chemistry again, at his age. The red and white cells blur, vanish into a quick chaos he stares into without blinking or understanding, until the image glows painfully white, and he turns away.

He rubs his eyes. Should he destroy his stock, go foraging in the winter cityscape for an untainted supply? It wouldn't be the first time, of course, he had had to destroy his holdings. Still, whether he takes the elevator or crawls down the side of the building (a fly on gray velvet), he prefers to avoid the lean pickings of winter.

He stands again before the freezer, sampling his supply until he locates the offending vintage.

.

Sometimes he dawdles with his memoirs. Tonight he recalls his evening with the historical materialist.

"We live amongst the ruins," the bespectacled professor said, his cheeks waddling. "The past is always tainted by the present. Surely you can understand that."

Indeed the vampire could. He liked this old fool he'd picked up after a recital at the Liederhalle.

The vampire offered his guest another helping of pasta and pesto (ground by the vampire himself that afternoon with a stone mortar and bowl, his own blend of pine nuts and basil and secret spices), then poured the professor another glass of the hearty Merlot the vampire had in ample stock.

"Wasn't it Walter Benjamin," the vampire said, tapping his aromatic cigarette into his barely tasted meal, "who said that we enshrine what we excrete?"

"No, no," the professor huffed, then paused and stared at his host. What did he see in my eyes? "I mean, yes, in a sense, but..."

"And wasn't it Benjamin," the vampire interrupted, "who whirled away on his dialectical tricycle until history, or the concept of the same, made a dialectical dish of him, somewhat like, Herr Professor Doktor Grillfustel, I am about to do with you?"

Still, that wasn't how he had wanted the evening to end. He, too, had desires, didn't he, that went beyond the material? He had wanted to let the professor linger for a few days before sending him away or finishing him off, but in the end—the final moment, the violent expulsion, the blast heard at the historical-materialist critical moment—the vampire could do nothing but drain his guest to the lees.

.

"I am conducting a poll," he says over the phone to Sadie Killpeck from Kansas who was spending a night in a hotel off Königsstrasse before heading off to Strasbourg to meet friends. The vampire chose the hotel and room number at random. "Do you believe the soul decomposes at the same rate as the body, only to be reborn, if only as, say, a flower or quantum dust?"

"Yes," Sadie Killpeck from Kansas said.

Hotel after hotel he called, asked for room number 42 and always the answering party said, "Yes." Yes, yes, yes. How lofty, how self-assured the living were. How quick were they to credit their thought with eternal form. He wanted to scream at them, he wanted them to learn his litany: What is Eternity? Dust. What is dust? Eternity. What is mind? Dust. What is dust? Eternity. What is Eternity? Dust. What is dust? Mind. What is mind? Dust. What is dust? The bowels crawling with worms, or just after. What is after? Dust. What is dust? Mind. What is mind? The gaping mouth, the tomb adorned. What is adorned? Dust. What is dust? A shudder. What is a shudder? The last. What is the last? Dust. What is dust? Eternity. What is Eternity? The mind. What is mind? The worms, or just after.

"Yes, Ms. Killpeck? You said, 'Yes'?"

"Yes," she said.

Later that night, before he put her on her train to Strasbourg, she said "yes" to him once more.

.

But on other days he stands before the mirror and sees nothing. Not that there isn't something to see, an outline, a shape, glass-gray eyes, but what are they if not nothing—nothing stretched thin as a string, a thread, bundled up and tossed into Eternity. It's been centuries since he's had to shave. Something in the blood, the transfer. The hair on his head, yes, that still grows, sometimes in long hanks overnight.

His favorite barber, an old Italian with a salon on Gutbrodstrasse, notices nothing. Around the vampire's head he clicks his scissors like castanets, then plunges in until there's only a quarter-inch of hair left. Then he vacuums the head with a hose, rubs it with his hand, and spanks it once, as if it were a baby's bottom.

And in truth, intoxicated by the hair oil and the music of the scissors, the vampire feels born again. He compliments Roberto and pays up. "Until next time, maestro," he tells the barber, bowing out, and the barber, gesture for gesture, word for word, repeats him.

Again at the window, at the window again, he sings to himself, a glass of wine in one hand, a cigarette in the other. An hour before dusk, but the sky is such a uniform gray it's hard to tell the time of day. It's snowing, of course, a drizzle-snow falling thickly on branches and roofs.

On the roof opposite him, a magpie scratches in the gutter for something to eat. Not three feet from the magpie is a dead pigeon, but the magpie pays it no heed. Instead it hops up the tiles with what might be a mouse or nut in its beak and begins to worry it. Still the dead pigeon is ignored. Who will come to take it away? No one lives in the attic apartment opposite. Magpies don't mind robbing a nest of its young, but a dead pigeon doesn't interest this wintry one. Most days, crows would be cawing their black heads off on the roofs and in the trees, but not today. Never there when you need them. Will he have to stare out all winter onto the dead pigeon, watching it decompose? The vampire scans the sky for a hawk or crow or some other carrion bird who might take it away, but the magpie alone moves amidst the snow falling on snow already fallen.

David Kammerzelt

Viewing

I took off my coat and threw it over the chair. No more livery. I unknotted my tie and threw it on the couch. No more wearing a noose around my neck. I unbuttoned my cuffs and rolled my sleeves up past my elbows. No more metaphorical manacles. No more outward signs of submission, none. The futile search for work was done for the day. Now was my time. I was meeting with Fern later that evening, and I probably should've been building myself up for the event rather than allowing myself to fall to pieces, but fuck it.

I disassembled onto the sofa, putting my feet up onto the coffee table that had never once supported coffee but that at this moment sported a motley collection of empty blue beer cans and green glass wine bottles and plastic soda bottles drained down to their dregs. I dug among the rattling empties to get to the TV remote, found it, and collapsed back into the thick couch cushions. I closed my eyes. My thumb found the power button on the remote without the guidance of my sight; the motion was written into somatic memory. I heard the sound that flooded the room but saw nothing. The rebroadcast sound of recorded explosions made the beer cans judder against one another. Their bases buzzed against the dirty glass of the tabletop.

I opened my eyes. A probably gay bodybuilder/action star with a stubbled head was placing his hands upon the svelte waist of and pretending to lock lips with a brunette model/actress. I clicked up one channel. A pretty woman in a seven-hundred dollar suit was telling me about how bad the economy was. As if I didn't know. I clicked up one channel. A pretty man in a seven-hundred dollar suit was telling me about how bad the economy was. I clicked up again.

How gay was gay? I wondered. If you had your hands on the hips of a woman who had, in spite of or perhaps because of her utter vacuity of personality, probably inspired at least one self-inflicted orgasm in each and every red-blooded heterosexual American male and the males of many other nations besides, would it do much of anything for you? Probably as much as it might do for me to have my hands on the hips of the probably gay bodybuilder/action star.

Click, click, click, the concept of "clicking" lingering on from a time when a the buttons were hard plastic and actually made sound when you pressed them but now the buttons were ergonomic soft rubber. The easier to thumb through eight ESPNs with, my dear. Click. I saw contextless clips of college basketball, a woman going through the motions of rolling out pizza dough as an excuse to show off her deep cleavage, more charts and graphics telling me about the terribleness of the economy, fluorescent cartoon goblins dancing to watered-down hip-hop beats and delivering choppy raps about how eating vegetables is awesome. And six-hundred or so more channels of the same. Each variation of nothing was more or less unique, but the general nothingness was the same.

Was it in the late 80s or early 90s that Bruce Springsteen had commented about how there were fifty-seven channels but nothing on? That was decades ago, of course. Now there were five-hundred and seventy channels. Same nothing, though.

I barely noticed that I had cycled through all of the channels and come back to the local networks. The only difference was that the freeways I saw on the car chases on the local had a vague familiarity to them, whereas the scenes of flooded Midwestern or Southern towns that I saw on the cable news were too abstract and distant to provoke much of a response from my thoughts or feelings.

Click. Click, click. Click-click-click. Click. The commentators, pundits, actors, and models finished one another's sentences, forming an overarching and senseless narrative. *Troubling news out of Iraq today: split ends and tangles got you down? Try our new miracle solution that is proven to I'm going to stick this gun down your goddamn throat and pull the trigger if you don't tell me "I'm not here to make friends, I'm here to win." All-new and improved, just listen to these ten eligible bachelorettes who are just dying to know whether biologists estimate that a total of forty-five thousand trout, bass, and catfish have washed up dead on the banks of the Chattahoochee river in recent days.*

It was only on my third cycling-through that I found it. I lingered for a full ten seconds on the acne cream infomercial on channel 381, watching a model who had probably never been ugly a day in her life pretend to have been devastated by unclear skin, and thinking about how she could be well-nigh covered in pustules and that she would still have access to exponentially more sex than I ever would. Click.

The digits in the corner did not display 382, but 381 again. I thought I had thumbed the button wrong and clicked it again. Golf was on 382. I watched a golfer stand around and not do much of anything for some moments before the image that I had skipped over in changing the channel started to register in my brain. I had changed the channel. There was something different on the screen when I clipped through it. I blinked.

I thumbed the channel down. The digits showed 381 again. But this was definitely not the acne cream infomercial.

It was striking in its lack of strikingness: a black silhouette of a man, from the shoulders up, centered against a grey background. That was it. The image didn't change. Accompanying the image was a tone, though it took me a while to hear it. The tone was at the very pitch of tinnitus, blending seamlessly into that grating buzzing that took precedence when there was no other sound to distract one from it. The tone didn't change.

I watched and listened for what must've been a solid minute. I kept expecting an abrupt edit to hypertanned women in crop tops bitching each other out or to a quarterback running in slow motion. But the edit never came. All there was was that silhouette like a hole in the light. That silhouette, set against that static background that was the color of cold ash. That silhouette and that background and that tone, that tone: that high, dry, cyclical whine.

The initial incredulity wore away, and I found myself wondering about the origin and purpose of the program. I found it hard to imagine any channel deliberately airing such a thing. It was hard to believe in this age of the rapid edit and the wardrobe malfunction and the reality TV throwdown that anybody would choose to air this unchanging, sexless image and expect to keep viewers around to endure the ensuing commercials. Or had the signal for some sort of public access avant-garde art program been misplaced to between channels 381 and 382? Had a channel or maybe the cable provider been hacked, and was this some sort of prank or stunt? That seemed more likely. Was it possible to hack a television channel? I didn't know. I didn't think so, but I wasn't sure. Or was it something else entirely? Hard to believe that any kind of electromagnetic interference could take on a constant shape, and that of something resembling the shadow of a man. Sunspots and lightning were too blind and mindless to exhibit that level of organization—weren't they? Or was I seeing the curious product of the one-in-a-trillion chance of the thing arising from nature that uncannily aped a phenomenon reserved exclusively as the product of human intelligence—the infinitieth chimpanzee at the infinitieth typewriter, the shadows on the mountain on Mars that when photographed at the right angle and with the proper lack of resolution collude to form a human face?

The phone buzzed in my pants pocket, startling me out of my thoughts. I fished the phone out, saw it was Fern calling, and then opened my phone and immediately clicked it closed again to terminate the call. Click. She could wait.

I got up from the couch and got down on the floor. I crawled around in front of the coffee table, the better to be able to study the image on the screen.

The shoulders were sloped, and the throat was long, and the forehead seemed foreshortened. Though one couldn't see any kind of definition within the outline, one rather received the impression of a man standing with his arms slack at his sides, his head tilted up and his mouth yawning, or maybe gaping or screaming. As though he were desperate with thirst and could do no more than to wait with an open mouth on the remote chance of desert rain. As though his last resistances had crumbled and he could do no more than wait, his body slack, for what horrors were to come. As though he were numbed by drugs to a point beyond caring. I don't quite know how or why these associations sprang to my mind, and I was a bit startled by them after I had them, but I nevertheless felt that there was some kind of accuracy to them, even if none of them suggested the entire truth.

I stared at the image, carving it into my memory.

That terrible fixity.

There. Just there, just now. If I watched the screen unblinking for long enough, I could see blurrings in the grey field at the edge of my focus, blurrings that suggested symbols. And I could hear oscillations in the tone. A pattern. A message— proof of some kind of communication, not just random madness. But I couldn't convince myself that these were not the projections of my own brain, seeking to impart motion and meaning on that grim, grey blankness.

That terrible fixity. That droning whine.

It was more deathlike than death itself. Death would be a mindlessness, would it not? There would be no caring. But here there was awareness and existence— the signal persisted—but these were broken in being utterly fixed. No variation, no progression, no possibility of change. That was, indeed, worse than an indifferent unconscious death.

My shadow, backlit from the lamp behind the sofa, fell over the TV screen. It fell to the figure's left side, the silhouette of my head falling just a bit below the figure's left shoulder. I scooted across the floor, adjusting my position so that my shadow overlapped with that of the figure on the TV I was only mildly surprised to find that the overlay was a perfect fit.

I watched. I waited, and I watched.

Mary Byrne

Rogues' Gallery II[*]

The immigrant

I am the black man your mother had expelled from the country because I frightened her and your family when I fell in love with you. Your skin was so pale and transparent I could see your veins through it. With your spectacles and your books you looked innocent, protected, sincere.

It was early 70s Dublin, you were in the city for the first time, away from home for the first time. She just couldn't let you go, accused me of harassment. Around drafty corridors, you and I talked about Kafka's *Metamorphosis* and what it might mean. I said the back of your hair was like an alluvial fan. You had optimistic ideas about racial equality, civil rights was in the air. We went to a disco at the College of Surgeons, full of foreign students. You fell in love with the music of James Brown.

The police told me your mother insisted on coming to the airport to make sure I was really put on the plane. The African, she called me. I spotted her there, thick-heeled and old-fashioned, in a sensible overcoat on a windswept day.

Now, they tell me, you are a 60-year-old spinster. You are very good to your parents, you live at home and look after them. I hope you look after yourself.

The nun

I am the former nun. Here in Female II they watch me carefully because they know that when I get going it takes half a dozen men to hold me down.

Last night was the full moon. I threatened the night junior with a broken bottle until she got through the window onto the fire escape and raised the alarm. Male staff rose from their slumber and came running, and the fun was over for another while.

---

[*] Mary Byrne was selected as the winner of *Fiction International*'s Spring 2011 contest on the theme of "Blackness."

The widower

I am the widower. The tax man sent me a bill for hundreds of pounds which I owe, he says, because my late wife's disability benefit, added to my income, pushed me into some new bracket, over some threshold. So I went out and got drunk and crashed the van on which I still owe thousands. It was my only source of income.

The late Mrs X, was how they put it in the letter. Her death was long, painful, expensive. She was distant yet very much there, barking instructions at me as I hobbled about tasks I wasn't used to. Women's tasks. Nurses came and went. I cut down my work to look after her.

It's not that I want her back as she was then. No, what I want is the smiling girl in the big album of photos that move from black-and-white to colour, taking her through fat and thin, from school uniforms to debs' balls. That's what I want back, not the gutted wreck she ended up. It was as if I'd got the chance to live her whole life with her, from 30 to 80, in the space of 3 years.

The late Mrs X.

Personally I think it's an insult to her memory to refer to her like that, but a friend says at least they got that right. Anyway, I still couldn't bear to talk about her to a man in an office—not about *The late Mrs. X.*

The wild man

I am the wild man who tore up tables that were nailed to the floor in Fusciardi's chip shop, the one you sent the police for. They roped and handcuffed me and took me to the Admission Unit. Staff gathered from all units to help nail me to the floor while the RMS injected me.

Enough to fell a Charolais for 48 hours, I heard them say afterwards.

The old flame

I am your old flame. This morning I came upon you in the supermarket. You were wearing a huge coat, looking larger than I'd ever seen you. Your blonde hair stood up on your head, set—you would no doubt call it—in a private bungalow on the edge of town, on the black, a nixer by the former assistant of the hairdresser who went bust.

There was a purple tinge to your face, unhealthy creases under your eyes.

'You're blonde,' I said, helplessly.

'Have to cover the grey somehow,' you said.

'How'ye Jeannie,' you called to a girl I recognized who'd been years behind us at school. She had that same cyanosed tinge, the same blonde hair.

When you shook hands to say goodbye, two of your fingers were curled, around a coin maybe, like an old lady of long ago.

I didn't look back as I went through the checkout.

The daughter

I remember her dressed up in a pale blue linen dress, with matching hat, gloves and bag. Then dressed down in the same dress for everyday work around the house, with an apron over it, a Craven A hanging uselessly in her mouth (she didn't inhale). When she wasn't smoking, she would sing 'The Whistling Gipsy'. Eventually she made the blue dress into a big laundry bag with drawstring that came with me to boarding school. Like many another less evocative item, I don't know what happened to it.

I did manage to keep one evening dress, the one she wore to a dinner-dance with Papa, in green and black brocade with a faint hint of Ponds Cold Cream. It fits me now but hangs in forgotten corners of the house, for no one goes anywhere in that kind of dress anymore.

The father

There's a photo of him as a young man in slacks and blazer, a rifle broken over his arm, in the middle of a field. He examines the photographer quizzically, his head slightly sideways. He was probably a newly married man at the time, but the wild thing is there behind that look, a wildness he later watched for in us all—and sometimes found.

The wild man grows old

I am their father. I am old now but they are still vigorous. They ask how I am doing.

'You're doing all right,' I told them yesterday, 'if you're fit to get your trousers on in the mornings.'

Dorothy Blackcrow Mack

The Black Cradleboard*

[Opening scene of *The Lakota Beaded Lizard: A Reservation Mystery*]

Camp Crazy Horse
Pine Ridge Indian Reservation, SD
May 1976, Day 1, Pre-dawn.

Alex Turning Hawk woke up before dawn in the old log cabin at Camp Crazy Horse and reached over for his wife, Tate, to stroke her hair. But the pillow was empty. Tate was gone. He remembered now, looking across the cabin at the empty spot where her piano had stood all winter. She was in town with Iná, his mother. Once she'd heard that Tate had morning sickness, Iná had come out with Big Al and moved Tate and her piano into her home at the housing circle in Eagle Nest. It happened almost before Tate could protest, and he knew better than to oppose his mother when she was on the warpath.

He'd stayed at the camp with his AIM *kolás*, American Indian Movement warriors, to keep the projects going, building log cabins and starting *Chanku Luta*, a Red Road to Recovery Center. They were cutting logs from the Tribal forest near the Badlands and hauling them back to Turning Hawk land, across from the sacred sundance grounds.

He pulled on his winter overalls and cowboy boots, picked up his sacred pipe and went out to greet the sun, just under the horizon to the east, sending rays into the bare poles in the sundance arbor, lighting up the tree of life in the center. A good day, a hard-work day. He turned to the west, toward the pines and called for his hawk—*kree–kree*—into the cool dry air, and began his morning prayer to the four directions, east to the sundance grounds, south to Rattling Water Creek, his source of water, then west to the pines, his source of lumber, and north to the Badlands wall, where Turning Hawk land dropped off into Redstone Basin.

Overhead he saw the dark shape of his hawk, circling, then sweeping down into the cottonwood tree near the creek below—*kree–kree*—buzzing him, strange odd behavior, rising, zooming in, then off toward the north, circling and returning.

---

* Dorothy Blackcrow Mack placed second in **Fiction International**'s Spring 2011 contest on the theme of "Blackness."

The hawk had come to him on his first vision quest when he was sixteen, when he'd been staked out to the wind and sky above the Badlands for four days and nights. Since then the hawk had become his constant companion. It was as if his ancestors had come to keep him strong, such as his great-grandpa who'd lived on this allotted land and kept his clan together in the terrible shoved-on-the-reservation days of sickness and despair.

The bird cocked an eye and listened as Alex shared his worries, fears, and plans for the day and the future of Camp Crazy Horse, AIM and his Lakota People. He could talk to no one else this way. With Tate, his American Indian buddies, and all those who came out to take sweat and ask for healing, he had to be strong and positive, patient and calm.

The hawk fluffed his wings, swooped down to perch on the woodpile by the door—*kree–kree*—as if he sensed Alex's heaviness, pulling him north, out toward the Badlands, something urgent out where his grandpa's vision pit lay.

Alex put away his pipe, picked up his work tools and flask of water, then closed the cabin door. He walked across the early-grass prairie to ground himself. Overhead the hawk flapped his wings and streaked off towards the top of the Badlands wall.

The spring air was so clear he could see Kadoka thirty miles away, the rising sun glinting off its granaries. And below, Redstone Basin's maze of barren arroyos twisted and turned as if forever. He stood on the edge of the world. The hawk buzzed him again then flew down next to the buffalo skull altar. Odd behavior for a hawk, not a magpie collecting shiny ribbons for a nest.

An odd buzzing came from the vision pit. Could be rattlers coming out of hibernation. He'd need to find a stick. Then the breeze shifted, carrying the smell of blood, decay and fear. Maybe some animal, crawling into the darkness to die. Definitely black flies buzzing, even though it was too early in the spring. He pulled his neckerchief over his nose and cautiously stepped past the old altar in front of the hide doorflap. The smell surrounded him and he hesitated. He'd brought only a flask of water along. Not enough to purify the sacred space. Maybe he should dig a new vision pit in the Badlands shale.

He put on his leather work gloves and lifted the doorflap. Black flies stirred and buzzed in the heavy darkness. No sunlight entered—vision pits always faced west—so he pulled the flap up on top and anchored it with a rock. He took off his jacket and whisked the flies out. Before him lay an old cradleboard with a beaded lizard bag tied to it for protection. Someone had made it to hold a baby boy's umbilical cord to remind him he was always connected to the earth. The beadwork was odd—pink beads, not the usual sacred colors. He reached down and lifted the headflap. Inside was a baby, his face turned black—not breathing, dead—wearing a black necklace—he leaned closer—no, a string of *wolutas*, cloth tobacco ties, but black not red. For a moment he thought he was staring at a life-size doll painted black, put there to scare him, but the fetid smell told him no. The baby and the black ties, each tie full of prayers, black prayers, were real. Evil.

He backed away, repelled, afraid. Questions clouded his mind. Whose baby? Dead how long? Why hide it here? Who else knew of this place?

Nothing made any sense. Only that someone had sent evil into the most sacred Turning Hawk spot, out to destroy him and his family. Iná, Tate, his unborn child. He looked around for his sacred pipe, his protection, but he'd left it behind. The spring breeze chilled him to the bone. His mind emptied. No prayers came to him.

At last he stirred, his face warmed by the sun. Medicine men weren't allowed to touch the dead. Yet he'd have to remove the cradleboard and baby, though he'd never wear the gloves again. He could bury the poor dead baby somewhere in the Badlands, but that seemed wrong. Someone had cared enough to bead a lizard bag for the baby, even if it hadn't protected him. He could turn it in to the Eagle Nest Tribal police and start a long complicated process, fueling the rumors already circulating on the res: so many Indian babies dying. The Moccasin Telegraph said so, and people were scared. Better keep this quiet while he searched for the person who killed the baby, or who let it die, who left it hidden for him to find.

He'd have to keep it secret. Of the remaining Turning Hawks, only his mother Iná had a strong enough heart to help him burn the black tobacco ties. Furious as she'd be at the threat to him, she'd keep quiet and bide her time. She'd know which clan had once used old pink beads. She might recognize the old-style cradleboard. And since she'd been a midwife for many years, she'd know what to do with the dead baby, maybe even figure out what had caused its death. Fortunately, she rose even earlier than he did.

He tore the hide doorflap loose from the vision pit and wrapped the cradleboard and baby in it. Chills shook his body as he carried the bundle awkwardly in front of him and ran back through the new spring prairie grass back toward his pickup. His neckerchief fell off, but he didn't stop. In his haste to leave camp before anyone else awoke, he slid the bundle in the pickup bed, then changed his mind and laid it carefully inside on the passenger seat. He drove without lights in low gear out to the road, then turned them on and drove into town, seeking the curtained light from Iná's kitchen.

Toby Olson

The Meal

Something out of the corner of the eye
or in the eye;
    something discovered in passing
[not nous in the passage]
within time spent in the concrete [a ladle,
a knife], recipes
fallen down from a bookcase.

The meal of the day is flanken:
    [Put meat in. And cover with water
or a little more than cover.]
blessings on the animal's flesh treated
so well in the preparation.
            And carrots in the corner of the eye
in time spent in the passage. And dumplings
formed carefully in the hands.
[Cook until meat
falls from bones. Constant skimming.]

And of course time passes in the treating
    [turnips in the corner of the eye
ripening]; remains of the animal passes
to a final destination
            [location possibly noted
in new growth], and we have come through
yet again.
    [Put carrots and dumplings in. Continue
until all is ready.]

Something in the corner of knowledge
[in the nose in the passage],
which is not knowledge
[in the great passage] formed
carefully in the hands, but flesh of the animal
treated to carrots and destination
[the only passage], through yet again
to rise up in the new growth
in the garden [eggplant,
basil and broccoli],
something out of the corner of the eye,
received in the eye
[the nose].

Blood of the passage in constant skimming
which is not nous but coming through
yet again partially changed
until all is ready. Something [a side dish,
wine, a ladle] in a corner in living,
a woman's knife and dumplings.

The meal of the days is discovered
in the corner of the eye's passage,
in the flesh heated to release scent
of garlic for the nose
[in the corner where a woman stands],
for the palm cupping the ear
to the bubble
[until the meat falls]
which is not skimming knowledge.

Fallen down from a bookcase,
ingredients of the careful lesson
[a recipe, a code, a knife]
gathered up from the floor of the dead
[location possibly noted]
given back into the corner of the eye,
not nous in the passage.

Seltzer on the table, a ladle, elbows,
compliments to the chef
   [into a fanfare], treated
to carrots and destination.

And of course time passes
   in time spent in the passage,
a simmer in the corner of the eye fallen
down from a counter,
recipes from a bookcase
there on the floor of the dead.
     Flesh of the beast as a burnt patient
the woman is carefully nursing,
   down in the scent of garlic,
anticipated skimming,
putting the meat in [casual sacrament]
out of the corner of the eye, caught
   partially changed
in the great passage [the only passage].
Cook until meat falls from bones,
until carrots grow vibrantly
dark orange color
   in time spent in the concrete
[wound that will not heal].

Yet again in the conversation
   [location possibly noted]
of new growth in the corner of the eye,
sacrament of the animal's passage
   within skimming of destinations
[garlic, a ladle, a knife],
fanfare of compliments
for the chef's knowledge [but not nous]
of blood breathing
   in the nose in the passage,
[desire for reversal of fortune]
in the nose in the passage
of blood breathing
for the chef's knowledge [but not fallen]
   fanfare of compliments

[up from the floor of the dead]
within skimming for destinations,
    sacrament of the animal's passage
of new growth
in the corner of the eye
in a garden of eggplant and tomato
        [location possibly noted]
yet again in the conversation;
the meat falls down from the bones,
carrots grow vibrantly
dark orange color
    [the wound that will not heal]
in time spent in the concrete.

Out of the corner of the eye caught
putting the meat in [casual sacrament],
in the great passage
    the woman is carefully nursing
flesh of the beast as a burnt patient
there on the floor of the dead
recipe from a bookcase,
a ladle in the corner of the ear fallen
    in time spent in the passage,
[the meal of the day is discovered]
and of course time passes
until all is ready.

[Flanken. Carrots and dumplings.
        Blessings on the animal's flesh
treated so well in the preparation
    and on the woman's hands in the corner,
a sacrament
fallen down among recipes from a bookcase,
the floor of the dead littered
    in the great passage] the only passage,
[ingredients of the careful lesson,
a conversation
    in the concrete, which is not knowledge.

Blood of the passage in constant skimming
of the meat put into a simmer
on the passage through
   to a final destination,
location possibly noted
in new growth.] And we have come
into the corner of the eye yet again,
partially changed.
Desire for reversal of passage
up from the corner of the eye's recipe
[casual sacrament],
   not fallen discovery. The floor of the dead
grows vibrant, garlic, a knife, a ladle,
     ingredients of the conversation,
fanfare: careful lesson [location
possibly noted] in new growth.

   And we have come through yet again.
Flanken. Seltzer on the table, elbows, a woman
brushing the floor of the skimming.
   Off in a corner of the eye,
a bouquet of carnations, a pot, a ladle;
the wine blood is breathing.
   It's getting late; time passes.
Let us begin the meal.

Gary Lain

Four Photo Sequence*

A young man with long, dark hair enters a supermarket.

It is 1971. Older-model American cars, with a few European imports, fill the parking lot. A jet flies high overhead, soundlessly, its white contrail stark against the hard, blue sky.

The young man prowls the supermarket aisles, passing the arrayed products—Alpo dog food, Crest toothpaste, Tide detergent. He notes their spatial arrangements, geometries and colors. He reads them as markers of the commodity culture.

Circling back towards the store front, he sees a young woman at a pay phone near the entrance.

It is 1971. People send each other letters, cards, photographs via the US Mail service. While on vacation they send postcards from Yellowstone National Park, Mount Rushmore, the Statue of Liberty, the Golden Gate Bridge. (Alcatraz Island has not yet become a state park and popular tourist destination. The abandoned prison complex, where imprisoned mobster Al Capone was stabbed by another inmate, is occupied by activists of the American Indian Movement.)

The young man passes down the frozen-food aisles, the corn and peas, popsicles, Tater Tots and orange juice behind frosted glass. He thinks of the ICBMs targeting Havana, Hanoi, Moscow, perched on super-chilled columns of rocket propellant.

He arrives at the meat counter, chicken and lamb chops, bacon and hamburger in refrigerated bins. He picks up a sirloin steak and stuffs it beneath his shirt.

The young man leaves the supermarket. He is photographed from outside of the glass door exit, eyes cast down, fluorescent lights reflected on the glass.

This is the first photograph in the sequence.

He walks to his car, drives home. In his garage he drops the steak into a chest freezer with the meat from previous forays.

115

The young man is engaged in conceptual art. Conceptual art is non-material, privileging idea over object. It is egalitarian, the low cost of materials requiring no government or corporate sponsorship. And because it is process-oriented, conceptual art resists commodification.

So shoplifting meat is art? Given the right context, yes.

Why meat? The meat invokes its means of production, which is wasteful, inefficient, environmentally unsustainable. The slaughter and butchery of the cattle is barbaric, and is performed by non-union, poorly paid labor, often by non-documented workers under harsh conditions.

When not working, the young artist goes to exhibitions (he sees David Cort's *Mayday Realtime,* an unmediated video recording of an anti-Vietnam War demonstration), reads, goes to the movies.

After several weeks of expropriating steaks, he defrosts them on the kitchen counter of his North Hollywood apartment. Friends come by, someone brings a jug of red wine, a joint is smoked.

The artist is photographed from the wrist down, clutching a steak in his right hand—the image describes an overdetermined sense of aggression. This is the second photo in the sequence.

At rush hour, he takes the steaks to the Hollywood Freeway, tossing them beneath the wheels of the oncoming cars and trucks. During a long gap in the traffic he runs onto the roadway to stand over a pummeled slab of meat. He is photographed crouching with left knee bent, thigh parallel to the road, left hand resting on his knee, his right hand clenched along second finger joints, a grimace on his face with eyes closed, as if a shout has been arrested. This is the third photograph in the sequence.

The fourth and final photograph is of oncoming traffic. A barren California hillside borders the background on the right-hand side. A semi-truck is cropped along the left front edge. Right and center of the image, a Chevrolet Impala rushes towards the viewer—two men occupy the passenger and driver's seats, perhaps the artist and an accomplice making their escape. The sky behind them is gray, flat, empty.

*Note: this text is based on an actual 1971 "performance," *Meat Theft/Disposal Piece,* by the artist Alan Sekula.

Eckhard Gerdes

Never Made Up

The Chronicles of Michel du Jabot
Book Three: Never Made Up
Part Fourteen—Blind and Deaf

After they left, I was alone. No more music played. The TV, which started to show *The Lady Vanished,* vanished. Vanished also were the accoutrements of Victorian England and even the byobus. I grabbed the beer out of the fridge before the fridge disappeared. But a minute later the beers disappeared. After the cell was emptied, the bars disappeared, and then the walls. Then everything beyond the walls. And then nothingness began to overtake me as well. My feet first, my ankles, calves, and then my fingers, hands, wrists, arms, thighs, shoulders, waist up, chest down. I disappeared at my navel.

Everything disappeared. No sound. No sight.

Move to the smooth. Working with the assumption that the more civilized one was, the smoother (like David Niven—I barely remembered his image! I hope it's not my last), I moved to the smooth. Rough would lead to sharp, dangerous; smooth to easy, comfortable. Of course a bowl evil can reverse the two—it's cotton—many (out of trouble) a time [a time again]. Trusted stet. Trust stet. The paper was high quality acid-free stock. My baby fell from a high class stork. A stute.

I stoop. Forgive me.

I just realized that the stork would be my last image, not David Niven.

Oh no, now it's Niven again. Niven in *Ninotchka.*

Thwack! A sign in Braille is slipped into my hands. It is from the literary police, who interject, <<Alliteration counts as sound! It can no longer be employed!>>

Neither should sound effects!

That would be rough.

Or groovy.

Yeah. Groovy.

I will not be able to hear the literary police anymore. It's all up to inner dialogue now!

Are exclamations permissible?

I don't know. Are questions? They both involve vocal inflection. No, only impassive demonstration is permitted.

You are taking a more formal tone. Certainly tone is a quality of sound.

Not once the signified has been separated from its signifier. The signified claims its independence.

Heck, she claims her humanity!

Who is she?

A beautiful soul trapped inside a uniform, unable to discard the garb because of a keen sense of obligation.

Is that sense visual or auditory?

I don't think so.

Okay, so the sense of obligation stays.

No, please—we'd be better off without it.

Why?

Obligation breeds resentment. Only giving freely frees giving.

You should make a bad motivational poster out of that.

Yep. Um. Well, no comment. What's a poster?

I—I don't remember. I don't even know why I said that.

Posters are the invisible who comment online.

Ah, good, so they're invisible. Then they cannot be visual. Superb.

Well, writing like this really goes against the grain.

It rubs people the wrong way. It's gritty.

It's a pain in the ass.

Harold Jaffe

Sacrifice

(*The Sacrifice* directed by Andrei Tarkovsky, 1986)

Barren windswept island off the south coast of Sweden.
Ingmar Bergman landscape.
Bergman's old colleague, Erland Josephson, plays Alexander, pensioner, former
writer with an unfaithful wife and young child, who is compelled to sacrifice.

His wife and child?

Himself.
His sole option.
The diseased earth is in the throes of dying.
Retreat or immersion.
No half-measures.
Retreat is illusory, immersion is sacrifice.

Does his sacrifice bear fruit?

He lies with the good "witch," devotee of Mother Mary.
He sets fire to his house.
He is forcibly restrained.
Transported to the institution where suffering is imposed.
Legislated torment.
But the war that would holocaust the diseased earth is nullified.
Time backs up.
Literally.
Temporary reprieve.

Why "temporary?"

Open your eyes.

Does it matter that Alexander is a failed writer?

Not failed. Ceased to write.
The joy—where there is joy—is in the art-making.
If that dies nothing remains but retreat or sacrifice.

Sacrifice imitates Christ whether or not it is fruitful?
Didn't Artaud, Sade, even Hitler, sacrifice in their own ways?

Not Hitler.
The other two—arguably.

Is the diseased earth irreparable?

You ask me or Tarkovsky?

Tarkovsky.

Man and his institutions will not cease to filthy o'er the earth.
Profiting all the while.
The diseased earth can be cleansed solely by God's grace.

Sacrifice?

Though not animals, not trees.
Not humans, unless the sacrifice is willed, chosen.

Did the "chosen people" will their "sacrifice"?
Their holocaust?

The Jews?

The Jews.

I think of Mahler, Jew despite his baptism.
   Mahler had the birds killed outside his dacha to claim the silence he needed to compose *Song of the Earth.*

That was the rumor.

Why bring up Mahler?

He comes to me.

What happens if one's sacrifice amounts to nothing?

Nothing happens.

It is the gesture that vibrates irrespective of results.
Even if the gesture costs your life.
But what if it costs the lives of others?
I think of John Brown's raid on Harpers Ferry—two of his sons killed. Brown hanged
for treason.

Weird John Brown.
"Weird" is Melville's word, meaning *fated.*
In Melville's poem the hanging shroud covers John Brown's face but not his
"streaming beard" which juts sideways foretelling the meteoric energy of the anti-
slave movement to come.

Slavery has not been abolished. It is everywhere in numberless guises.

Yes.

It is the process not the result we are discussing.
Yours is a bleak view of the world.

Made world.
The world itself—what remains of it—is a blessing reviled.

Old Testament.
You sound like weird John Brown.

Without sacrifice.

Why without?

I could have made my opportunity but hesitated.

Back in the day you considered joining the Weather Underground.
Considered becoming a "human shield" in the Palestinian territories.
Considered joining the flotilla delivering supplies to blockaded Gaza.

I grieved from a safe distance.

You know about Pasolini's homosexual relations with rough young boys in the Rome ghettos.
Maybe you heard the odd story?
That he deliberately provoked the boys to beat and murder him so that the debased photo with his face battered, trousers at his knees, sex exposed, would testify to our squalid globe.
Presumably he envisioned it as a sacrificial, or better, shamanic act.
Weird story, but in Pasolini's instance, not implausible.

I admire Pasolini however he choreographed his death—if that's what he did.

How does one distinguish narcissism from sacrifice?

They can be indistinguishable.

You are a writer sans frontiere.
Doesn't your writing count?

Count?

As a species of sacrifice?

I don't know.

Contributors

Jonathan Baumbach's 16th volume, *Flight of Brothers,* will be published by Dzanc in 2013.

Guy R. Beining's most recent visual books include *Out of the Woods into the Sun* (Kamini Press, 2011) and *Measurements of Night III* (Marimbo Press, 2011).

M. Benedict is a writer, editor, and friend to those accounted mad. He awaits the end of human days in San Diego, California where he fantasizes about a world inhabited solely by birds.

Kenneth Bernard's *From the District File* was recently published in France under the title *Extraits des archives du district* and will be published in Spain in 2012. Five of his Wittgenstein Poems were just published in *Little Star 3.*

Originally from Chicago, **Jackson Bliss** earned his MFA from the University of Notre Dame where he was awarded the La Vie de Bohème Literary Award and the 2007 Sparks Prize in Fiction for his debut novel *BLANK.*

Gerald J. Butler has published fiction and poetry in a number of literary magazines, including *The Hudson Review* and *Fiction International,* and has presented many papers in Europe and the United States on the theory of the novel, especially as exemplified in works of the eighteenth century. He is currently writing fiction.

Mary Byrne, born in Ireland, is a French-English translator living in France. Her short fiction has been published in Europe, North America, and Australia. Anthologized stories appear in *Faber Book of Best New Irish Short Stories* (Faber 2008), *Queens Noir* (Akashic Press 2008), and forthcoming in *Best Paris Stories.*

Cyril Dabydeen's stories and poetry have appeared in more than 60 literary magazines as well as the Heinemann, Oxford, and Penguin Books of Caribbean Poetry. His novel *Drums of My Flesh* was nominated for the IMPAC/Dublin Literary Prize and won the top Guyana Prize for Fiction, 2007.

Eckhard Gerdes is the author of 13 published novels, including *Hugh Moore and My Landlady the Lobotomist.* His tetralogy *The Chronicles of Michel du Jabot,* of which the included piece is an excerpt, is nearing completion. He is also the editor and publisher of *The Journal of Experimental Fiction.*

Harold Jaffe has published 20 books of fiction, docufiction, novels, and essays. His most recent volume is a collection of essays and quasi-essays called *Revolutionary Brain.*

David Kammerzelt is a writer living in Southern California.

Evelyn Kelly lives in San Diego and has published fiction in numerous literary journals.

Gary Lain lives in San Diego, California with his wife and two young sons. He has published fiction, reviews, and essays in *Fiction International, The Journal of Experimental Fiction, Review of Contemporary Fiction, The Texas Review, American Book Review, Belphegor, Crash Test, City Works,* and online at *Locus Novus, The Brooklyn Rail,* and *The Sixteenth Letter.*

Joel Lipman's introduction to Bern Porter's *Found Poems* (Nightboat Books, 2011), "The Sciart Origins of Bern Porter's Found Poems," can be found online at Sybila and through PIP (Project for Innovative Poetry). His Porter photographs are web sited at *Jacket2.* He is currently researching patterns of erotic desire in Bern Porter's personal correspondence. Representative work from Lipman's sequence "Origins of Poetry" is online at The Poetry Foundation. He is Poet Laureate of Lucas County and lives in Toledo, Ohio.

Dorothy Blackcrow Mack is a contributing editor at *Calyx* and past director of Writers on the Edge. She has writings published in *Folio, Fireweed, The Literary Review, Shaman's Drum,* and numerous anthologies.

Andy O'Clancy reads theory and fiction and writes fiction and theory.

Toby Olson's most recent books are the novel *Tampico* (University of Texas Press) and *Darklight* (Shearsman). He is currently working on a short story collection.

Shane Roeschlein is a writer, activist, and musician who lives in San Diego, California. His texts have appeared in *The Journal of Experimental Fiction, Pacific Review, Mighty Mercury,* and *Fiction International.*

Ryan Seslow is a multidisciplinary artist, independent curator, and professor of fine art living and working in New York. He has displayed his art nationally and internationally.

Norman Simon is a retired professor of astrophysics. His stories have appeared in *Bellingham Review, Center, Hawai'i Pacific Review, The Literary Review, The Massachusetts Review,* and *New South.* Recently, he has completed a novel, *Thoronet.*

From 1964 to 2006 **Charles D. Tarlton** taught political philosophy at the university level in Berkeley, San Diego, Victoria, B.C., Christchurch, N.Z., and, finally, Albany, New York. Now he devotes himself entirely to poetry. His wife, Ann Knickerbocker, is a painter, and they live in Oakland, California.

Joseph Triscari has been creating one-of-a-kind illustrations for nearly 10 years. Stemming from these illustrations is his printing company Moon Light Speed Press where each hand-drawn illustration is used for a variety of projects, from screen-printed concert posters for local and national musical acts to large outdoor murals.

Mark Wallace is the author and editor of more than fifteen books and chapbooks of poetry, fiction, and essays. He teaches at California State University San Marcos.

Tom Whalen's books include *Roithamer's Universe, Dolls,* and *The Birth of Death and Other Comedies: The Novels of Russell H. Greenan.* He teaches American literature at Freiburg University and film at the State Academy of Art and Design in Stuttgart, Germany.

Please consider subscribing to Fiction International for $16, making a tax-deductible donation (of any amount), or purchasing one (or more) back issue:

EDITION #	PRICE		EDITION #	PRICE
44 (DV8)	$16.00		23 (Visual Art Against War)	$7.00
43 (Walls)	$16.00		22 (Pornography & Censorship) DOUBLE ISSUE!	$14.50
42 (The Artist in Wartime)	$16.00		21 (unthemed)	$7.00
41 (Freak)	$16.00		20 (American Indian Writers)	$7.00
40 (Animals)	$16.00		19.2 (AIDS Art)	$6.00
39 (Abject/Outcast)	$12.00		19.1 (Third World Women Writers)	$6.00
38 (Sacred/Shamanic)	$12.00		17.2	$8.00
37 (War/Resistance)	$12.00		16.1	$7.00
34 (Madness II)	$12.00		15.2	$7.00
33 (Madness)	$12.00		15.1	$7.00
32 (Sabotage)	$12.00		10/11 (Asa Baber)	$5.00
31 (Terror[isms])	$12.00		8/9 (Robley Wilson, Jr.)	$5.00
29 (Pain)	$12.00		6/7 (various)	$3.50
25 (Mexican Fiction)	$10.00		4/5 (various)	$3.50
24 (Japanese Fiction)	$7.00		2/3 (various)	$3.50

Please include $2 postage (domestic) or $4 postage (international). To order by credit card, please go online to www.fictioninternational.com and order using PayPal, or make your check out to *Fiction International* and mail it to us at:

Fiction International
Department of English
San Diego State University
5500 Campanile Drive
San Diego, CA 92182-6020

Revolutionary Brain • Harold Jaffe

In this timely collection of essays and "quasi-essays," acclaimed novelist and critic Harold Jaffe explores the intricate vicissitudes of millennial culture. Gesturing, in a philosophical shorthand, toward a kind of pop Armageddon, *Revolutionary Brain* is at once thesis, allegory, and surreal comedy, demonstrating just how far we, and the natural world we have debased, have fallen.

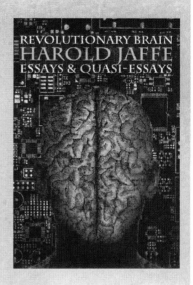

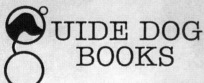

www.GuideDogBooks.com

The Kyoto Man • D. Harlan Wilson

In the third and final installment of the Scikungfi trilogy after *Dr. Identity* and *Codename Prague*, acclaimed author D. Harlan Wilson composes a narrative grindhouse that combines elements of science fiction and horror with pop culture and literary theory. Erudite, ultraviolent, and riotously satirical, The Kyoto Man reminds us how, at every turn, reality is shaped by the forces that destroy it.

www.RawDogScreaming.com

www.KyotoMan.com